DON'T READ THIS BOOK AFTER DARK VOL. 1

A HORROR ANTHOLOGY

ALICE J. TAYLOR   BRIDGET EILIS

LUCILLE BANE

NEIGHBORS

BRIDGET EILIS

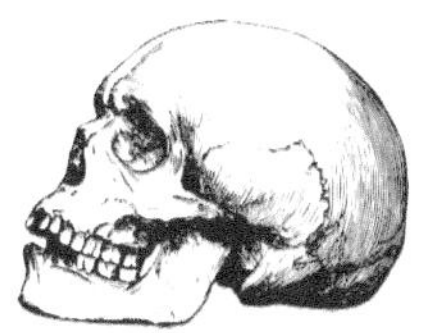

WHEN WE MOVED INTO OUR NEW HOUSE, WE WERE PREPARED for an older than average neighbourhood population. The houses on our new street were all legacy buildings—some had even been designated as historical landmarks. Our real estate agent had enough notes to make up a small history book when she was showing us around.

She didn't have to sell us on it though. My husband, Chris, and I had always dreamed of moving into a creaky old house. The older the better. Chris had secret dreams of finding a haunted house that no one else would buy and somehow getting an amazing deal. I suspect he's watched a bit too much TV.

Not that we ended up over-paying for the house we were currently moving boxes into. It had been on the market quite a while, and the selling agent was very eager to get rid of it. They accepted our first offer, even though it was well below asking price, no questions asked. We were ecstatic. Just being able to buy our own home in only our late twenties had become something of a pipe dream. But I couldn't stop myself from browsing, and one day had stumbled across this Victorian beauty.

It needed work—like a lot of work—and I was reasonably sure now that we were putting boxes and furniture on the floor that we were disturbing the oldest dust I had ever encountered. I vaguely wondered what sort of crap we were currently inhaling into our lungs, but then I was distracted by the beautiful hardwood and vaulted ceilings and I ceased to care.

The moving guys dropped off the last of the big stuff in the large dining room off the foyer, where we stacked everything that we didn't know exactly where to put yet. Chris fished his wallet out of his pocket and stepped over to the doorway where they patiently waited, sweaty and dirty just like us, for their payment. When he was done, we both bid them a seriously grateful goodbye. I looked around at all the boxes and heaved a sigh of relief that we had only had to actually move a fraction of it. Definitely worth the money.

"Come here," Chris beckoned, arms outstretched. He pushed the door shut against the scene of aging foliage on the street and wrapped his arms around me. "We're home," he said.

"I know!" I replied, squeezing him around the waist. I couldn't contain my giddy excitement. He lifted me up in his strong arms and spun us both around.

"We did it babe," he whispered in my ear. We kissed deep for a long moment before pulling apart, both gasping. "Okay, initial celebration over, let's unpack some dishes so we can eat in the next day or so eh?"

I laughed in response, my head thrown back in glee. "Agreed."

While I dug through all the boxes labeled "kitchen" trying to find the most essential dishes and cooking utensils,

Chris headed to the local grocery store to stock up on supplies and a celebratory bottle of wine. A loud knock interrupted my excavating and I wondered who could possibly be at the door—we'd only been official residents of this neighbourhood for a few hours.

I pulled back the heavy wooden door, making a mental note to head down to the library and see if they had any building records or if city hall had permits filed. I'd love to find out just what kinds of wood were used throughout the building.

Is there such a thing as a wood type tester? I thought, grinning at my own absurdity.

On the wide front porch stood a couple who, to my surprise, looked to be even younger than Chris and I. I was sure the demographics reports I'd read had pegged the average population age at closer to sixty five years. *Maybe they are someone's kids, or grandkids.*

I realized belatedly that I was standing there with my eyes wide staring dumbly without saying anything. Thankfully my wonderful husband came to my unintentional rescue, pulling into the driveway at that very moment and drawing all of our attention.

Three sets of eyes turned towards Chris at the sound of gravel crunching under car tires. *Is It my imagination or do they look really excited to see someone they don't even know? Maybe they are just friendly and I need to get over my city person's snobbiness.*

I smiled brightly at my approaching husband. "Look, I found the neighbours! Or rather, they found me," I said, turning back to greet our guests properly, hoping we could just skate right past my earlier awkwardness.

"Hello," Chris said as he reached the steps. He juggled the grocery bags into one hand so he could offer her other to shake. "I'm Chris, and this is my wife Samantha, or did you already know that?" He cocked his head to the side, looking between them and me as he shook first the woman's hand, then the man's.

"Nope, hadn't made it that far yet," I said with a nervous laugh, offering my own hand. The too-young couple still hadn't said anything, their bright eyes oscillating between us with almost alarming speed.

"Tabitha," the woman finally said as she shook my hand in return.

Holy crap her hand is freezing. She drew the word and handshake out a little longer than was strictly necessary, this whole encounter was becoming weirder by the second. Even though all we had done was say hello, sort of. It felt like we'd been standing around for ages and we still only knew one of their names.

"Johnathon," said the man, after another long moment. He held my hand just a beat too long as well, in his equally freezing cold hand. His eyes were a weird colour. I realized that I was staring at them but I also didn't stop, until Tabitha started talking again and I wrenched my gaze away from Johnathon to give her my full attention.

"We just wanted to stop by," she said, "and welcome you both. To the neighbourhood."

"Yes," Johnathon added, "it's been so long since we've had, since anyone new has moved in." Tabitha shot him a look, one I couldn't read, but didn't look pleased.

"We'd love to have you both over for dinner," she said, "once you're settled in of course."

"That would be nice," Chris replied. I seemed to have lost the ability to form coherent sentences—my brain felt foggy. "I do need to just," he stepped between them towards the door, "get these groceries in though." He used his free hand to turn the knob, swinging the heavy door inwards with his foot.

"Yes, of course, we won't keep you," Tabitha said, grabbing Johnathon's hand and leading him down the stairs quickly. "We'll come back in a day or so to make arrangements, shall we?"

"Sounds good," said Chris. He dropped the groceries inside and reached for my arm, gently tugging me into the house. I crossed the threshold and shut the door, and the whoosh of air and dust being displaced tickled my throat and I coughed. The full force of the weirdness that had just taken place hit me like a truck.

"What the fuck was that?" I asked no one in particular. "Were they really strange or was it just me being an awkward weirdo?"

"Well you're always an awkward weirdo hun," Chris replied, scooping up the groceries bags from the floor and heading for the kitchen, "but they were definitely...different."

"They were very intense," I said, following him so I could help put the groceries away and pilfer snacks while I did it.

"It felt like they were moving in slow motion," Chris said, pulling boxes and packages out and setting them on the counter.

"It rubbed off on me," I said. "I felt like I was underwater or something." A shiver ran up my spine and I tried to shrug it off. *I'm just tired, sore and hungry. There's no need to start ascribing weird personalities to the first two people we've met. I need carbs that's all.* "What did you get for dinner?" I asked, changing the topic completely, Chris seemed to be of the same mind as I was and latched onto the dinner topic with fervour.

"Come see for yourself," he said, and wrapped his arm around my waist when I stepped beside him to inspect our haul. "I got all your favourites, dining room floor picnic sound good?"

"Sounds perfect," I replied and kissed him on the cheek, the strange new neighbours already forgotten at the prospect of our first meal in our new home.

FOUR DAYS LATER, we were elbow deep in boxes working on unpacking all of our books. The kitchen had been the first room we'd gotten done, as it was the most essential to survival. Unpacking is easily the best part of moving, picking new homes for all your things. But it also results in your house looking like a small cardboard and tape filled bomb has gone off in each room.

I stood surveying the built- in bookshelves, trying to decide where to start. *Sort by author? Or alphabetically? Or alphabetically by author?* When I heard the heavy front door rattle in its frame, *knockknockknock,* the noise rang through the house.

"I got it!" I called to Chris, wherever in the house he was. I was pretty sure he was hiding out somewhere to avoid book sorting under the guise of unpacking another room.

This time I wasn't surprised to see Tabitha and Johnathon standing on the other side of the threshold.

"Hi guys!" I said, "How's it going?"

"We are well," Johnathon replied in his slow motion voice, "yourself?"

"Oh, we're great!" I replied with a bright smile. "Neck deep in empty boxes and dust bunnies, but still great."

"Neck deep you say, you've been busy these last few

days," he replied, and Tabitha elbowed him lightly in the side.

"Of course they've been busy Johnathon, they just moved in," she said. "We thought today might be a good day to have that meal together, what do you say?"

"Oh uhm, sure I guess," I said. "Let me just ask Chris." I turned and hollered my husband's name into the old house. As I suspected, he came jogging out of our room off the upstairs landing, our room that was already unpacked, the slacker.

"Sup?" he asked from the top of the stairs, then, "Oh, hi guys. I can't believe I didn't hear the door." He reached the bottom and stood to my side, one hand on the small of my back.

"They want to know if we wanna do dinner tonight?" I said, gesturing between ourselves and the couple outside.

"Oh, sure I don't see why not," he said. "What time? And should we bring anything?" Chris turned his attention to our neighbours waiting patiently, so still they seemed to be barely breathing.

"That's not necessary," Tabitha said with a slow smile.

"Just bring yourselves," Johnathon added, "shall we say seven?"

"Sounds good, we'll be there," said Chris.

"Just uhm, where is there?" I suddenly remembered that we didn't actually know where they lived, I just assumed when we met them that they were nearby.

"Oh, how silly of us," Tabitha said with a laugh, and for the first time since I had met her she seemed normal. She pointed to a house just a few doors down from us. "We're right over there."

"Ok great," I replied. "We'll see you at seven then, you're sure you don't want us to bring anything?"

"Quite sure," Johnathon said, and they stepped off the landing and headed down the driveway.

WE BOTH THOUGHT the polite thing to do would be to shower off the dust and sweat before heading over to someone else's house, so we spent the rest of the afternoon digging through our bags of clothes for something decent to wear and getting clean. By six forty-five we were both ready to go, standing in the foyer together.

"Is it weird that I'm nervous?" I asked my husband, squeezing his hand.

"No," he said, returning my squeeze with a reassuring one of his own, "making new friends and moving to a new town are butterfly-making activities." He turned and smiled, melting my insides.

"Shh, be quiet with your logic and rational thinking," I replied, leaning up on my toes to press a soft kiss against his mouth. "Shall we?" I opened the door and stuck out my elbow comically waiting for him to take it. Instead he pushed me out the door with a light shove and a laugh then turned around to lock the door behind us.

"Remind me to pick up new locks at the hardware store next week," he said as he turned the heavy old key in the ancient lock, probably still on the door from when the house had first been built. "Who knows how many people might have a key to this door floating around out there."

"Good call," I said. "I promise nothing about reminders though, put it in your phone." I skipped down the stairs to the driveway while Chris mock-scowled at me and tapped his phone screen a few times.

"Done," he said, pocketing the device and following me down, we headed out towards the street together.

We reached Tabitha and Johnathon's front door in just a minute or two—it really was just a few doors down. Being such an old neighbourhood, the lots were bigger, but the houses still weren't that far apart. They had a creepy brass door knocker set in the middle of their front door.

"Am I supposed to use this thing?" I asked Chris. "Or is it just like, decorative?"

"Oh I'm totally gonna use it," he replied and reached for the heavy metal loop, banging it against the door three times.

The door swung open so fast I wondered if they were waiting on the other side for us.

"Welcome," Tabitha said, "please, come in." She gestured with her arm in a sweeping motion towards the inside of their house, oddly formal for a dinner with neighbours, but whatever. I had resolved to stop judging them for being so weird.

Chris crossed the threshold first, tugging me behind him by the hand. I stepped across and couldn't hold in my gasp. The inside might have been straight out of an historical documentary. All the furniture and drapery matched the age of the house, deep maroons and plush velvet. It was an historian's dream.

"Omigod, your house is gorgeous," I gushed, all apprehension about their strangeness forgotten as I wandered into the sitting room off the foyer. "Where did you get all this period furniture in such good condition? It must have cost a fortune!"

"Oh, we like to collect *old* things," Johnathon spoke as he entered the room through a set of double doors on the other side. I tried not to jump out of my skin—I hadn't heard him coming at all, which seemed impossible in such an old house that must be full of creaky floorboards and rusty hinges.

"Well I'm so jealous, I love old stuff," I said. "That's why we bought our house actually. We couldn't believe the price for such an awesome piece of history."

"Do you hear that Johnathon," Tabitha said as she and Chris followed me from the foyer into the sitting room, "she loves *old* things." She let out a delicate laugh.

Is that funny? I thought, running my hands over the sumptuous cushions on a fainting couch set up under one large window. I looked up from my examination of the fabric to see Johnathon standing directly in front of me. *Jesus, how does he move without making any noise?* I straightened up and took a step backward without really understanding why, but I suddenly really needed to get some space between us. Unfortunately the window was right behind me, draped in heavy deep blue blackout curtains that softened the blow when I backed into it.

Johnathon seemed oblivious to my discomfort, or was he enjoying it? He stepped around the fainting couch, closing the distance between us. It was then I realized for a brief, fleeting second that there was no smell of food cooking in the house—weren't we supposed to be having dinner in just a few minutes?

My heart pounded in my chest and I wrenched my gaze away from the man looming in front of me to find Chris, his eyes also wide with panic, staring at me from across the room as Tabitha held one slender hand around his throat. I tried to call out for him but fear choked my voice so that when I opened my mouth all that came out was a soft mewl of terror. Johnathon laughed.

"Don't be afraid dear, we'll teach you all about the *old*

things," he said, a simple sentence that somehow sounded sinister. My eyes were drawn back to him—now he stood practically on top of me. Close enough that I should have been able to feel his hot breath against my face, except he wasn't breathing.

He grinned at me, baring teeth that were impossibly sharp, and the last thing I thought was, *No fucking way,* as he sank them into my throat, piercing deep and spilling my blood into his mouth.

THE END OF THE RAINBOW

ALICE J. TAYLOR

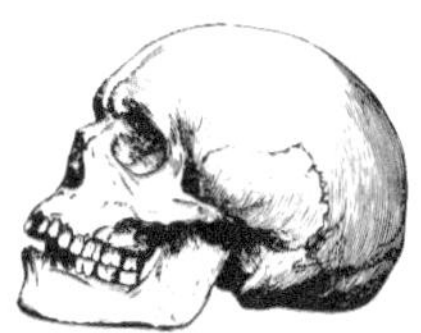

PIPER BLEW A SWEATY BLONDE RINGLET OUT OF HER FACE. SHE felt like she was breathing soup in this humidity.

Mallory squealed with excitement from up the trail. "There's a stream just ahead!"

Piper picked up her pace, and crested the hill just as her friend splashed into the knee deep water with glee. Piper all but flew down the hill and ran in, relishing the cold sting on her toes. She knelt down and immersed her arms, and then dunked her head.

Upon surfacing, Mallory trilled out a laugh and wrung out her short strawberry locks.

"Ahhh." Piper let out a noise of satisfaction and sat down on the slick rocks below, her body temperature at a significantly more comfortable level.

Mallory leaned over to fill her water bottle and then straightened up, putting a hand on her delicate hip. "Shouldn't be too far now!"

Piper sighed, curling her arms around her knees. *A nice hike in the forest would be relaxing, you said. Oh what a pretty rainbow, let's see what's at the end of it, you said. It'll be fun, you said.*

They'd been walking for an hour in what felt like a thousand degree heat, and Piper certainly wasn't having fun. She wasn't even sure where they were, but Mallory had assured her she knew this forest like the back of her hand. She just hoped they'd get to the end of this stupid rainbow soon, so she could go home and curl up with a coffee and some TV, which was how she'd wanted to spend her Saturday. That was her idea of relaxation.

Piper had humoured her friend, figuring the stupid rainbow would disappear and they could turn around. But the thing was persistent. She assumed it was the humidity providing enough moisture for it to linger...however, she couldn't deny that it felt like magic.

"Okay, let's go!" Mallory bounced on the balls of her feet like a kid waiting outside of a candy store.

Piper forced a smile and joined her friend, squeezing her sopping clothing so they wouldn't be so heavy. She twisted her hair into a quick braid and stretched her arms high above her head, letting out a loud groan as her muscles warmed back up.

Soon the forest grew denser, the trees closer together, absolutely no semblance of a path remaining.

Mallory slipped between two sturdy branches. "Do you hear that?"

"Hear wh—" Piper stopped short.

It was a low hum, a buzz, like a swarm of a thousand bees. Her chest tightened and a brick formed in her stomach. The tiny hairs on the back of her neck stood on end, and electricity danced up her spine.

"It's beautiful!" Mallory breathed, and picked up her pace, weaving through the trees with the grace of a dancer.

Piper caught a branch just before it smacked her in the face. "Define beautiful."

The noise grew louder. Were they getting closer, or was the noise moving towards them? It no longer sounded like bees. More like...*people* making buzzing noises. Thousands of people. But here? Deep in this random forest?

What the hell is out here?

"Mallory..." Piper lost sight of her friend in the thick flora and her throat tightened. "Mal!"

She suddenly, most certainly did *not* want to know what was out there.

All at once the hum stopped, and Piper heard her friend laughing. She struggled through the thick branches, and tumbled out into a clearing.

The rainbow touched the earth in the centre of a thick ring of daisies. Piper gawked at the sight of her friend frolicking with all kinds of animals. Bunnies and ponies and squirrels, raccoons and robins and even large cats. Jumping, playing, and dancing.

Her feet rooted to the spot, the daisies nearly blinded her with the whiteness of the petals. It was beautiful.

Or at least, it should have been. But something felt...*wrong.*

"Mal," she called, but her voice came out hoarse, dry, the name cracking into dust as soon as it left her mouth.

Her friend didn't even acknowledge her, and Piper clenched her fists. Her heart *thunked* in her chest.

She'd need to go in there.

She took a deep breath and stepped forward. It felt like she was dragging her feet through mud. As if the very air were pushing her back.

She finally stepped over the row of daisies, something shimmered, and then she was on the other side.

A long-toothed beast with giant bunny ears and rheumy sick eyes stood next to the rainbow, one of Mallory's legs clamped in its jaws, blood spurting from the ragged thigh like a dying spring.

No no no no no no—

A slithering snakelike creature with thousands of tiny humanoid hands sticking up out of its back like scales gnawed on her best friend's beautiful face, the head now severed and slick with viscous fluid.

Piper fell to her knees beneath the inky blue sky, the rainbow bleeding into the earth like lava.

She couldn't scream or move or think as the beasts all froze. Simultaneously, every monstrous head turned towards her, breathing putrid steam in her direction. A feral cat with too many legs grinned, revealing a raptor's mouth and a long forked tongue.

As it lunged for her soft flesh, Piper found that she could, in fact, scream.

THE BOOK

LUCILLE BANE

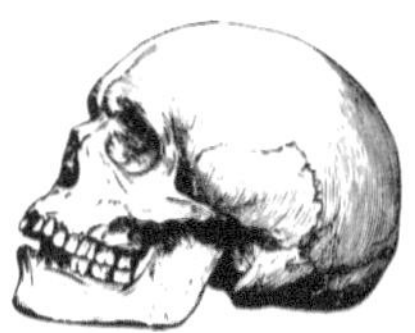

I DON'T EVEN KNOW WHY I WAS IN THE LIBRARY THAT DAY. Seven years I've lived in this town, and it was only the second time I've been inside. Something drew me in that day, and I would soon discover what.

The noise was deafening, louder than a plane taking off. The shelves shook with a fury that knocked nearly all the books loose. I thought it was an earthquake, despite the fact that the town was nowhere near a fault line.

It had to be an earthquake. After the tremors stopped, there came a noise that was almost unexplainable.

It was a roar, a gurgle, a rush, an angry Fist of the Gods. The building shook again, but not a tremble or a rattle this time. One hard raging shake that knocked me off my feet. As if a freight train hit the wall at full speed and full capacity.

My concerns about finding an engaging True Crime book were completely forgotten as I stumbled to my feet, tripping awkwardly over the fallen tomes. I raced to the nearest window, oblivious to the fact that there may be injured or frightened people in the building.

Looking through the glass brought me no answers, for

what I was seeing couldn't possibly be real. The street was gone, cars gone, houses roof-deep in water. It was impossible! We were deep inland, nowhere near an ocean or even a large lake. Only water here was a small river that snaked through town. Little more than a stream so shallow and tame that young children waded to the centre to hunt for frogs and minnows. It had never been a threat even in the wettest seasons.

I needed to find a person. I needed to find an answer. I tore through the library despite having no idea where I was going. I sprinted down hallways, leaping over fallen shelves with more grace than I'd ever possessed.

Eventually, I found myself at the bottom of a flight of stairs facing a heavy wood door. I didn't even think to question why the library didn't flood. It should have been under the water line, yet the concrete floor was completely dry.

Something urged me to go in that room, even though I was supposed to be looking for other people. I heaved the heavy door open and stepped inside. It was warm, dry, dimly-lit and sparsely furnished. Only a desk and a worn-out chair sat in the huge book-filled space. There were hundreds of books, most of which appeared to be journals. I picked one up and gingerly flipped the pages, confirming that it was handwritten.

I suddenly felt strangely overwhelmed with this discovery and sank into the ratty chair. Impulsively, I opened the desk drawer without knowing why. A small journal of black snakeskin with silver edged pages slid forward. It felt important. I picked it up and carefully opened it to the front page.

It read:

1891

The life and times of Maxwell Fletcher

My heart pounded in my ears at this unexpected coincidence.

That was my name, but written a hundred years before my birth.

Curiosity mounting, I began reading. With increasing horror, I found it was a play-by-play account of my life. I flipped forward until I found an entry titled *The Dam Burst*. I skimmed the pages, reading a perfect depiction of my day so far. When I reached the end I realized there were more pages in the book.

Did I dare continue reading?

OL' MISTER SCARECROW

ALICE J. TAYLOR

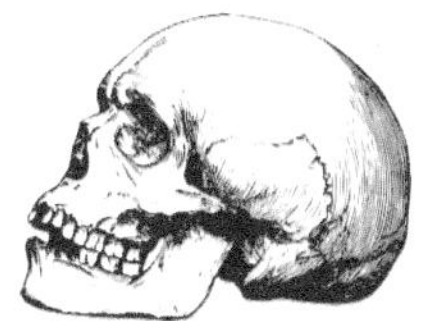

Ol' mister scarecrow has been in my family for generations. Countless Wilsons have lived on this farm, and the story goes that my great-great-great-grandfather put together this scarecrow with his own two hands. Oh, it's had different outfits over the years, but it's the same jute head and stained face.

The same wood, too, somehow. I know they didn't have ways to treat their wood back in the day, but somehow this guy's never rotted out. He's weathered rain and sleet and snow and tornadoes. It's amazin' really.

My granddaughter don't like ol' mister scarecrow. She says that she feels like he's watchin' her. I told her that he was, he was watchin' the whole farm, protectin' it from predators. Then my daughter-in-law got in a hissy with me because that seemed to scare the little one more.

Thankfully my son smoothed over that debacle. He says that his wife wants to get rid of the scarecrow when they inherit the farm. I guess it's for the best, if he's gonna be scarin' the little one.

But ol' mister scarecrow's got a few years yet. I'm still spry enough to take care of the farm.

At the end of the day, I tip my hat to him, and head inside. I eat my TV dinner and watch late night game shows until it's time for bed. I brush my teeth and get into my plaid pyjamas, glancing out over my little cornfield one last time.

He's there, standin' proud right smack in the middle of the field, keepin' watch over my crops.

"Thanks and g'night, ol' mister scarecrow."

THE NEXT MORNING, I roll out of bed, my old knees cracklin' and my back stiff. I give a big ol' stretch, my arms up straight in the air, and utter a loud, satisfying groan. As I stand up, scratching my left ass cheek, my eyes narrow.

"Did you move overnight, mister scarecrow?" I ask.

No, that's ridiculous. He's a frigging scarecrow. But I swear he was a little further back last night. I shake my head. My eyes ain't what they used to be.

I work my way through my morning routine, all the way to heading out to the porch for a morning pipe an' coffee. Instead of sittin' on my rockin' chair, I decide to take a stroll over to see mister scarecrow.

We've had to move him a few times. Usually he's good right in the middle, but sometimes the birds'll get brave and pick a corner of the field and we have to move him a little off to the side. But it's been at least two seasons since we've had to do that.

I reach him and bend down to check the post. The earth around it is solid, as if the wood had grown right up out of it. I grunt as I straighten back up, and take a deep sip of my hot brew as I study him. Faded denim overalls, a red plaid shirt.

His clownish face, painted shit-knew how long ago on the straw-stuffed burlap that makes up his head. And up on top, the frayed woven hat that I'm pretty sure came from a thrift store.

Maybe I'd been wrong. Maybe this was where he was the night before. I mean, musta been, right? Damn thing couldn'ta just got up and walked over here. Unless my kid is playing a prank on me. But to drive all the way out here in the middle of the night to fuck with mister scarecrow? Somehow I don't think his old lady would be okay with that.

I scratch the back of my head. "I'm watchin' you."

IT'S NIGHTTIME AGAIN. In my flannel plaid pyjamas, again. Sitting on the edge of my bed, facing the window, again.

He's closer. I swear to fuck he's closer to the house. Not just that he moved last night, either. He's closer than he was that morning. Am I really losin' it? I grip my bedspread. Should I go out there?

Fear grips my chest, and I just don't know. I'm not usually such a yellow-belly, but I've been here all damn day and there's no way anyone could have snuck around to move him, unless they managed to do it while I was brushin' my teeth. But how? So fast?

I ain't goin' out there. It's not even cause I'm scared, either. There's no point in goin' out there. What could I do? Tell him to move back? Tell him to stop it? He's a damn scarecrow.

I'm going to call my son tomorrow and chew him out. It has to be him.

"Hey, dad, I was going to call you tod-"

I growl into the phone. "Why you been movin' the damn scarecrow on me, Billy?"

"What?" He pauses, and there's a shuffle, as if he's shaking his head. "What are you talking about?"

"The scarecrow!" I snap. "You been comin' over when I'm not lookin' and movin' him! Two nights ago and again last night! When are you doin' it? And why? Stop it! The crows are gonna get the far corner now, since he ain't in the middle!"

"Dad, chill," Billy replies slowly. "I haven't been to your place since we visited a week ago. I wouldn't come sneaking around with the scarecrow. Come on."

I scowl at the phone for a moment, and then look back out the window. He's even closer than he was the night before. Closer and closer to the house. If Billy's not doing it, then who is? I hate how on edge this has me.

"Dad?" my son asks, so gentle that I want to snap at him again.

I'm not some crazy old coot that doesn't know what he's talking about!

"Nevermind," I finally say with a sigh. "Musta been some of the boys from the farm up the road. You know how teenagers can be. When are you gonna bring my granddaughter around to visit me? I miss her."

It's quiet for a moment, and I know the damn kid is evaluating whether or not I've lost it. "We can come by on Saturday," he finally says. "Lena has to work but Gigi and I can come out for lunch. You want us to bring some burgers?"

"Yeah, get that cholesterol flowin', eh?" I force a laugh. "See you on Saturday, son." I purse my lips for a second, and then turn away from the stupid scarecrow. "I love you."

There's a small noise of surprise on the other end, and I

wince. Has it been that long since I've said that to him? I should say it more.

"I love you too, dad," he says, and then I hang up before I start to worry him even more.

Ol' mister scarecrow is closer tonight. When the hell is he moving? I need to just sit here, on the side of my bed, staring out this window, do a stakeout, that's it. I'll catch whoever is doing this. Or if the damn thing is just pulling his fuckin' pole out of the ground and moving himself. I have to know. I have to.

Maybe little Gigi is right. Maybe he is creepy. His smile looks bigger. Is it my imagination, or does he look happier? No, not happier. That's not a happy smile. It's a fuckin' cheshire cat grin. It's an *I'm gonna eat ya* grin.

Dammit I am not a young punk gettin' scared over stupid little things. Why am I givin' myself the willies so bad? This is stupid. I'm going to sit here and watch, with all the lights off, and by the light of the moon I'm gonna figure out who's playin' this damn prank on me.

My head is fuzzy. I squint. It's still dark. But I fell asleep, sometime. I'm cold, even though I've got my warm jammies on. But I'm on top of the covers, sideways on my bed. I look up at the ceiling, the full moon casting a rectangle of light there.

Suddenly I'm freezing, my muscles seizing and my blood pumping ice through my veins. There's a silhouette of a man in that rectangle of light. I sit up straight, stock still, and my eyes nearly bug out of my head.

"M-mister scarecrow..." I stammer, because it's him. He's standing right outside the fuckin' window. How? How is this happening? There's nobody else there. I know this, somehow, as my gut clenches and my bladder gives way, a hot stream of piss soaking my jammies and the bedspread below.

Oh, he's grinnin' alright, with a full set of razor sharp teeth.

BILLY WALKS THROUGH THE FIELD, somber. It's his field, now. Inherited the farm from his dead father. He's all moved in, but little Gigi won't come outside to play until the scarecrow is gone. Lena's told him to get rid of it. She said if the birds get at the corn then they'll just put in a flower garden instead. Who needs this much corn, anyway?

He frowns as he approaches ol' mister scarecrow, and I don't blame him. He's been in our family for generations. At least I know, as he reaches inside to pull the dank straw from my insides, that one day I won't trap him on this post like my daddy did to me.

THE LUCKY ONES

BRIDGET EILIS

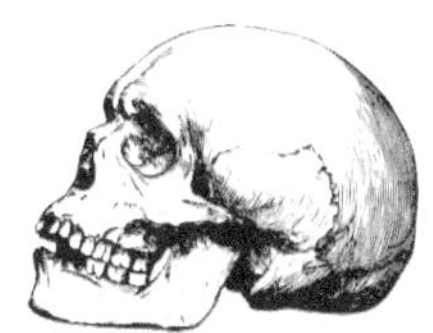

IT'S BEEN FIVE YEARS SINCE THE END OF THE WORLD. IT CAME in a way no one was expecting. Except maybe the most absurd conspiracy theorists. It wasn't a plague or nuclear war. It wasn't climate change. It was zombies. Fucking zombies. Brain eating, slow moving, unkillable zombies. Just like the damn movies.

It wasn't supposed to happen this way. It wasn't supposed to happen at all. But it did. They came out of nowhere. No country or government could pinpoint the origin. Not that the governments lasted very long. The *problem,* as we called it now, happened overnight. Within days they were everywhere. People were being converted at an alarming rate.

I was one of the lucky ones. If you can call it lucky. I was still alive anyways. The survivors had gathered in small groups, populations of fifty to one hundred people. We managed to hold them off. Usually just by virtue of where we happened to be when the *problem* began. Those in the most defensive places were able to band together and survive. Until The End.

The End was when the zombies suddenly dropped dead, or dead again. It happened several months after the first reported instances. One day they all just dropped. Right where they stood. Collapsed to the ground in heaps. Some survivors had been in the midst of being attacked when it happened. They were the real lucky ones. Escaping death by mere instants.

We've spent the intervening years rebuilding. Civilization that is. The buildings themselves are still intact. Most of them are still standing. It happened so quickly. There wasn't time to get any bombs or missiles off. Not that it would have helped. The zombies were everywhere all at once. Bombing any one place would've done no good. Except to kill innocent people. Which may have been a better end for most of them I guess.

Corpse removal was the worst part. They started to rot very quickly. Being undead as they had been before The End, decomposition didn't take long to set in. And when it did, it made life more unbearable than it had already been. But we'd gotten past all that. The streets were clear, at least where we lived. The farms were producing food. We'd made radio contact with others. They seemed to be in basically the same situation. Civilization as we knew it was over.

There was no coming back from this. Maybe in a hundred, two hundred years. But not for us. For us this was what there was. Survive, like we'd always done. Like we'd been *lucky* enough to do. I still wasn't sure how I felt about that word. Some believed we were the blessed. The chosen. The ones who were picked to move on. I knew better.

We were the damned. And just how damned we were became apparent the very next day. The ships descended all at once. Eerily similar to how the *problem* had spread from everywhere at once. We poured out into the streets.

Everyone staring at the sky as one. It should have been easy to accept one impossible thing. Especially after you've seen other impossible things. But it wasn't. It never gets any easier. I stared at the descending spacecraft.

What the actual fuck? First zombies, and now aliens. Was I living in a goddamned video game?

They hovered there, doing nothing for a solid day. We came and went from our houses. Taking turns to double check that we weren't all experiencing some mass hysteria induced by extreme trauma. That didn't seem to be the case. The ships just hung there. Doing nothing. Taunting us with their presence. With the threat of yet another insurmountable problem. Hadn't we given enough? Hadn't we paid our dues?

I was surveying the crops when it happened. Bright lights erupted around the town. Each one disgorging an alien figure. Definitely not little green men, that's for damn sure. They came down in heavy duty armoured suits. They stood at the end of every street. Unmoving, threatening again just by their mere presence. As unofficial leader of our particular group of survivors, I swallowed my fear and headed towards them.

I stood in front of one for a solid minute. It said nothing.

"Hello," I said. "Can we help you?" It seemed absurd. Shouldn't they want to see our leader or something? But I didn't know what else to say.

"Greetings...human," it replied.

"Greetings," I said. "Can I ask what the fuck you're doing on our planet?"

"There has been an error," it said.

"Error?" I asked—what the actual fuck is my life right now?

"There was to be no one left. How many remain?" it asked.

"Remain?" I replied, confused. It couldn't be.

"Since the end of life," the alien replied.

"The end of..." I couldn't finish my own thought. This couldn't be. It couldn't. What happened was a freak occurrence. A virus or something. I couldn't believe that someone would do this to us on purpose. No.

"We are sorry that you have remained. It was not supposed to be this way. We require your planet. We are sorry." The alien was still talking. I had a hard time registering its words. It wasn't until I noticed the weapon that I realized.

We weren't the lucky ones.

PRECIOUS

ALICE J. TAYLOR

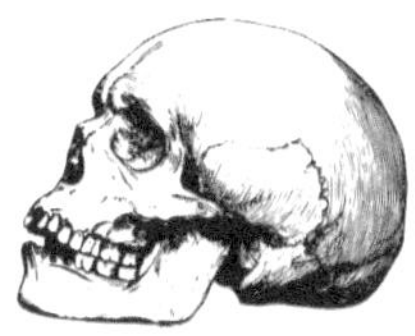

CARL'S BLOOD RUNS COLD WHEN HE SEES THE CHERRIES IN THE rear view.

Fuck. Fuck.

His stupid old sedan can't outrun a cop car.

Heart pounding, he eases the car over to the shoulder. He'd taken a country route to avoid attention, gone exactly the speed limit, and all his headlights are intact.

Why was this cop out here, choosing him?

Stay cool, Carl. It's just a routine check, just stay cool.

The cop takes his sweet time walking up to the car, and when he taps on the window Carl realizes it's a chick cop. Of course. Bitches in uniform with something to prove to guys like him.

Stay cool, Carl.

"License and registration?" Her firm tone leaves no room for nonsense, and he hands his credentials to her. "Been drinking?"

"No, ma'am," he says.

She barks a humourless laugh. "Ma'am?" She shakes her head. "Christ." She hands back his papers and he's sweating.

She stares at him.

What? He swallows.

"Can I..." His mouth is dry as sandpaper. "Is there anything else?"

"No," she replies. "Have a good night." She smirks. "Sir." She smacks the top of his car as she walks away, making him jump.

He lets out a shaky breath, about to groan in relief, when he sees her freeze in his side mirror.

The trunk gives a mighty *tha-thunk.*

Shit.

She pulls her gun.

Shit fuck.

Before he even thinks twice, Carl tumbles out of the driver's seat.

The cop yells at him, but it just sounds like screeching to his panicked ears.

Tha-thunkthunk.

She reaches for the trunk handle.

"Don't!" he screams, holding out his hands in a futile attempt to stop her.

She points her gun at him, eyes like steel. "Stay back!" She pulls her radio and holds it to her lips. She's saying something about backup but Carl is in a daze, heart on the pavement, dreading her opening the trunk.

Thunktha-thunkitythunk.

"Please, don't." His plea is shaky and quiet and his lungs collapse as she opens the hatch.

"What the—" She breaks off into an inhuman squeal.

Carl watches, white faced, as tentacles and teeth devour her, the sounds of sickening bone crunching, slurping, and grunting bouncing around in his skull.

The creature pauses for a moment as if to burp, and Carl

uses the momentary distraction to leap on the hatch, slamming it down on the creature. It shrieks, pulling most of its tentacles back inside, severing two in the process.

Carl lays on the closed trunk, chest heaving, tears running down his face.

Fuck. Fuck fuck.

Thunk! Wham! Tha-thunk!

Sirens bleat in the distance, and he scrabbles across the asphalt to leap back into the driver's seat.

He punches the gas. "Time to get you out of here, precious."

THE HOUSE

LUCILLE BANE

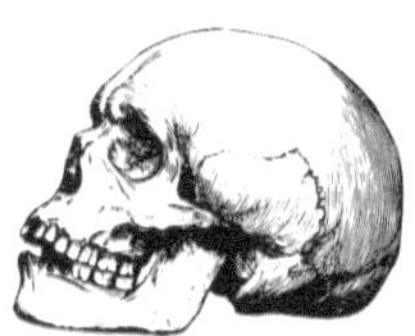

I HATE THIS HOUSE. I DESPISE THIS HOUSE.

Everyone who's ever set foot in this house has fallen in love with it. Its high ceilings and exposed wood, four bedrooms and three bathrooms, complete with hardwood floors and clawfoot bathtubs. The backyard was nearly the size of a city park, meticulously landscaped, boasting gazebos and even a damn koi pond.

This is the house everyone dreams of. Everyone except me.

This house holds my nightmares, my pain, my fears, my ghost. I want to sell it—I *should* sell it. A house like this, in this city? I would walk away a million dollars richer, which at 29 years old, would be life changing.

Yet I can't. I made a promise, despite the fact that I always hated this house.

You see, this house is haunted. Or, perhaps, I'm haunted.

It's not just the occasional bump in the night, as old houses are prone to do. There's the voices, familiar voices, whispering to me. They call out and taunt and tempt me. If the voices weren't enough, there's the other things.

When I turned the formal sitting room into a home gym, I returned from work to find all the mirrors smashed, the treadmill track shredded, all my bands snapped.

I've called the police, of course. So many times that they no longer send units to this house. There's never been any forced entry, no missing valuables, no evidence of anyone being here except me.

The last cop suggested I needed professional help. I thought he was right, so I went. I sought help. I told the therapist everything. She treated me and tested me for everything. Eventually, she declared me mentally stable. After all, I'm a successful investment banker in the prime of my life, with a sunny outlook and a thriving social life.

Except when I'm in this house.

Things had been escalating for a while, and as I sat on the porch that sweltering July night, I found myself seriously considering selling.

"Don't you dare! You promised," a familiar voice hissed in my ear.

I nearly fell out of my chair at the sound of my mother's voice. I gritted my teeth before answering. I hated talking back to my mom, even now. Especially now.

"I know I promised, but I can't do this anymore! It's too much. I hate this house."

I heard her stomp her foot on the solid wood porch, in that way that was unmistakably hers. "No," she snarled.

Suddenly there came a cry from deep within. A child's cry, a cry I remembered well, that shook me to my core.

"Randy?" I called out. "Randy, where are you? Let me help you. Just tell me where you are."

The cry grew in volume as I inched towards the centre of the house.

"No." I stopped suddenly, knowing where I was being led. There was a forceful shove at my back, making me stumble a step forward, closer to the basement stairs.

"NO!" I screamed, even as I felt myself being tugged forward.

Down the stairs I went, one shaky step at a time. The familiar crying was nearly deafening now. Hot tears stung my eyes, yet I couldn't force my legs to stop. I reached the bottom of the stairs and flipped on the light. I turned around and ducked beneath.

I had never been under here, not in all my 29 years living in this house. There, set back in an alcove, was a dark mahogany door, bound tightly in chains. I stared at it, both scared and resentful.

Anxiety washed over me like a tidal wave, and I slid my hands into my shorts pocket.

"Oh, come on," I groaned as my fingers closed over a key that definitely was not there a moment ago.

"Go," my mother whispered, shoving me again.

Reluctantly I unlocked the padlock securing the chain, hands trembling and sweating.

The crying had stopped, no longer necessary to lure me deeper. The chains dropped free and I put a gentle hand on the door. It swung open as if on casters, far too easily for such a grand thing.

I steeled myself against my fear and stepped inside. The lights snapped on as I sank to my knees, not even noticing the door close firmly behind me.

In front of me was an enormous room, filled with tables. On each one lay my nightmares, perfectly preserved and untouched.

My grandparents, who died in the backyard, struck by lightning on a perfect sunny day.

My little brother, Randy, mauled by a stray dog while playing with his cars on the porch.

My father, run down by a drunk, while mowing the lawn on a Tuesday morning.

My mother, who died in agony in the master bedroom, from a disease no doctor could diagnose.

My fiancé, the light of my dark life, crushed by his car in the garage while changing the oil.

Impossible, I thought, having watched them all get buried in the family plot. Yet here they lay, solid, pristine, real. I couldn't bring myself to touch them, but I didn't need to in order to know I wasn't hallucinating. I scrambled for the door, searching for the knob. After a solid minute of absolute frenzy, I accepted there was no knob. This side of the door was smooth and untouched.

"I hate this house!" I sobbed as I sank to the floor and the lights clicked off.

8

SCALES

ALICE J. TAYLOR

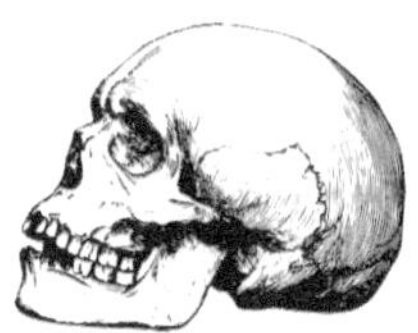

I MUST BE DREAMING. I WENT TO SLEEP IN MY ANIME PYJAMAS and now I'm weighed down by something heavy. I run a hand over my chest, fingers trembling over iridescent green scales. My heart leaps into my throat, and I have a brief moment of panic in thinking that I've become a lizard before I realize that I'm wearing armour.

My legs are covered in the same scales, all the way down to my shiny boots. My hands are free, however, and I snatch up a sharp stick from the ground.

I jab my palm with it. Hard.

Ow.

Not dreaming, then.

I clutch the stick to my chest as if it were a talisman, and look around. I'm standing in what only can be described as a hallway, the walls navy blue and opaque. They're shiny, like glass, and glint as I shiver with fear.

They're so high. I look up and I can't even see the sky. Just dark blue glass, stretching into the distance until it looks like it just meets in the stratosphere.

The ground is just dirt. I have no idea where the stick

could have possibly come from, considering there are no trees. Just dirt and glass, and green scales.

I turn around, and there's a dead end there. A sign hangs on nothing, as if by magic, appearing to be solid gold with embossed letters.

You have one hour. Don't touch the walls.

One hour until what? And now I really want to touch the walls. I mean, I kind of wanted to touch them before, because despite my fear and confusion, they're beautiful. But why would the sign tell me not to?

Argh.

Okay, self. Think. The only logical explanation in this highly illogical situation is that I have to get out of this place within an hour. It's clearly a maze. And if I don't... then I wake up? Hopefully?

Panic blooms in my chest, and I shove it down into my gut, stamping it down as hard as I can.

There's only one direction to go, so I grip my stick and start walking. Years of playing first-person shooters have taught me to sweep my eyes everywhere as I move. Though I'd feel much safer with a rocket launcher right about now.

I don't know why I feel that I need a weapon. As far as I've seen, I'm alone. But with everything I need to worry about right now, it just seems smart to have one. My spine tingles.

I don't know how much time has passed as I turn left and right, but there's a pressure in the back of my skull as the seconds tick by. I speed my brisk walk almost to a jog.

How big is this maze? I would be less bogged down without this armour, but I don't want to waste any time trying to figure out how to take it off. And I can't shake the sinking feeling that I'm going to need it.

I'm not wrong.

I turn a corner into a large round area, and instantly gag at the stench. I swallow bile and then choke on it at the sight of an absolute monster.

Miles of slick skin oozes translucent brown muck, legs sticking out every which way like branches. It turns a catlike head towards me, and its mouth opens to reveal thousands of putrid, rotting teeth.

I'm rooted to the spot as it skitters along the ground, my panicked brain taking in the mesmerizing precise landing of each speared foot.

I shake myself. I don't want to get eaten. But I can't go back the way I came, and the only other opening is on the other side of the monster.

I grip my stick, what had been a talisman suddenly feeling like a needle compared to the thing, and I will my legs to move.

It slings a speared leg at me, goo flying everywhere, and I shriek as I dodge.

Don'ttouchthewallsdon'ttouchthewallsdon'ttouchthewalls...

I scramble desperately, leaping and ducking and avoiding the wet squelching of the monster's attack as I try to get around it. I dive over a sweeping leg, and finally I'm clear, I'm on the other side, and I sprint for the corridor.

Warm slime splats against the back of my neck and I pitch forward, eating a mouthful of dirt.

I dig my fingers into the ground and try to propel myself upwards, but my boots are slippery with pungent gunk and I slide headfirst into the wall.

I'm curled up in a little ball, and I slowly get to my feet, realizing faintly that the smell of the creature is fading.

Wait, what creature?

I must be dreaming. I went to sleep in my anime pyjamas and now I'm weighed down by something heavy. I run my free hand over my chest, fingers trembling over iridescent green scales. My heart leaps into my throat, and I have a brief moment of panic in thinking that I've become a lizard before I realize that I'm wearing armour.

My legs are covered in the same scales, all the way down to my shiny boots. My hands are free, however, and I snatch up a sharp stick from the ground.

I jab my palm with it. Hard.

Ow.

Not dreaming, then.

9

THE MIRROR

BRIDGET EILIS

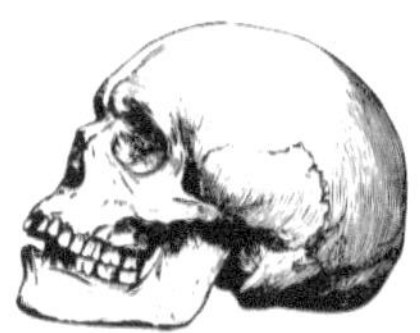

IT STARTED WITH TAPPING. NOT INCESSANT, AND NOT ALL AT once. But from the day she moved in, Melissa heard it.

It's just the house settling, she told herself. It was an older house, after all. She'd gotten it for a steal; the previous owners were incredibly eager to move out. There had been rumours swirling about the family for months before they put their house up for sale. Their missing teenaged daughter, the fact that no amount of police investigation had turned up any evidence. Eventually the case had been closed, classified as a runaway situation.

Old houses are prone to creaks and strange noises, she told herself as a reassurance. There was no pattern to the tapping noise, and no discernible origin. Everywhere she went she could hear it. Stranger still, everywhere she went, it was the same volume. It didn't quiet as she passed through the rooms. Closing doors did nothing to dampen the sound.

Tap tap tap tap taptaptap tap.

It wasn't enough to make life unbearable, just mildly annoying. But things continued as normal. At least for a while. Until it wasn't just tapping.

When the hissing started, Melissa began to suspect something might be wrong with her new-old house. She searched it from top to bottom, even venturing up to the rickety attic that she avoided for fear of falling through the ceiling. The house inspector hadn't found any problems with the floors up there, but it gave her the creeps just to walk under the trapdoor in the ceiling. She hadn't even stored anything up there, and when she checked she found it reassuringly empty.

She hired a plumber to check all the water lines and pipes. A gas line technician to check for leaks. Neither of them found anything wrong, but more disturbing was the fact that neither of them could hear the noises. She watched the plumber as he made his way through the house on Monday, waiting for him to ask about the *tap tap taptaptap* and occasional *hsssssssss*. After half an hour she was peering at him so intently as he inspected her toilet that he stopped and turned his gaze on her.

"Did you need something miss?" he asked, a perturbed impatience evident in his voice.

"Can't you hear that? Don't you wonder what it is?" she burst out in response, her arms flailing wildly.

"Hear what?" he replied, his impatience giving way to confusion.

"The—" Melissa stopped herself just in time, before the poor plumber thought he had walked into a crazy person's house. "Nothing...thought I heard something. Must've been a bird," she finished hastily, and high tailed it out of the bathroom, leaving the perplexed plumber to finish up in peace.

Even worse was when the gas man came to check the lines. She let him in and stood expectantly to the side of the open door, so focused on waiting for him to mention the noise that she forgot to close it. Eventually the young man reached and eased the knob gently from her grip, eyeing her warily as he swept the door closed.

"So...what seems to be the problem?" he asked, and Melissa finally snapped out of her intense focus when he took a visible step away from her.

"Problem?" she replied, head tilted to the side, "There's not really a problem per se, well except...never mind. I just moved in and I wanted to have the lines checked, just in case, you know."

"Ahh, I see," he replied, smiling now, "that's a smart idea ma'am. I'll just get to it then." He headed off to check the natural gas in the kitchen and pipes coming in through the basement.

Melissa had to physically restrain herself from following him through the house and when she tapped her debit card on his portable machine to pay him, inside her head she was screaming, *Don't you hear that?!*

Friends that came over also claimed to be unable to hear the noises. One friend even suggested that maybe her house was haunted. Melissa laughed out loud at the prospect—she was reasonably certain that ghosts did not exist. Still, she was desperate to find a physical explanation. Something that would explain where these noises were coming from. But as more time passed, she began to worry that she was losing it, and considered making a doctor's appointment to have her head examined.

That was, until she heard her name.

IT WASN'T TOO late on a Tuesday evening. She remembered the day specifically because it's not every day your house begins calling your name. Deeply engrossed as she was in the movie she'd been watching, she jumped clear off the couch when she heard it. She slept with the lights on that night.

The next day found her engrossed in her local library with every book on ghosts and poltergeists that she could find. Being scientifically minded made it difficult for her to accept that something supernatural might be occurring in her own home, but she couldn't deny the sounds she was hearing. At this point, the joking suggestion of a friend from just a few days ago seemed more and more likely to be the only possible explanation.

Tapping she could attribute to a loose shingle, knocking in the pipes, a branch hitting a window. Even the hissing could be hand waved away as a possible slow leak, maybe not in a gas pipe but in a hot water pipe somewhere maybe. But the very distinct sound of her own name being called? What else could that possibly be?

In the back of her mind, the story of the missing teenager from the previous owners had taken root and blossomed into a paranoid delusion. Had they done something to their daughter after all? Was her ghost haunting Melissa now, unable to rest until her murder was solved. She had pored over the newspaper articles from the investigation, but there really had been absolutely no evidence of foul play. And the family involved had been distraught, but maybe they were just really good actors.

She was not ready to confront the idea that she might be ill, though the idea of visiting a doctor continued to loom in the back of her mind. Mental health issues ran in the family, something she had steadfastly avoided thinking about for most of her adult life. Watching her mother's descent into late onset schizophrenia was a terrifying thing to live through. Especially given the genetic component of the disease. The nagging reality of a scientific, though thoroughly depressing explanation, continued dancing around the dark recesses of her mind.

So, Melissa became convinced that there was a paranormal explanation. Abandoning all her previous pragmatic beliefs rooted in science and solid evidence. She grasped at any straws she could find. She approached various priests for advice on exorcisms. This generally ended in the various holy men trying to convert her to their particular brand of faith before even entertaining the idea. Only after her continued begging for help would they explain to her, gently as though talking to a child, that exorcisms don't exist anymore outside of movies and history books.

She even went to see a psychic, which turned out to simply be a waste of money, as she was told all about her very vague future. Lots of clichéd comments about darkness in her future and stuff that sounded like it was straight out of a trashy horoscope. Melissa was tempted to peek under the table and see if the lady was reading from a card of generic predictions, but the smell of incense started to choke her throat and nose. She had reluctantly paid the woman and exited via a gauzy and bedazzled curtain doorway.

All through this, the noises continued, but no matter who she had to come examine the house, no one could hear them but her. She lay in bed, thinking about the doctor a concerned friend had recommended. The number was written on the notepad on her nightstand.

She placed her cell phone on top of it, determined to call in the morning and admit that something must be wrong with her. Loathe though she was to have reached that conclusion, she had exhausted every other thing she could think of. And if she were being totally honest with herself, it had all been a stall tactic to avoid getting to this point.

THAT WAS the night that the mirror appeared.

She stared at the ceiling, unable to sleep, contemplating the implications of all the mental illnesses that involved auditory hallucinations. Chances were, she was experiencing the early indications of schizophrenia, the same as her mother had. But in between her research of all things occult, she had ventured cautiously into the terrifying world of medical research.

What she found had not been reassuring and only spurred her on to find some other explanation, even if it meant that all the things that go bump in the night were real. All these thoughts chased themselves through her mind, round and round, making her head spin as she prayed desperately for sleep. She tossed and turned for hours, eventually coming to resent the glowing red numbers on her alarm clock. Eventually, she just turned the stupid thing face down to hide the time, angry at the clock for allowing it to slip by as she remained unable to sleep.

She was desperate for sweet oblivion where she could escape the voices and noises at least for a few hours. Finally drifting off, her eyes grew heavy and that's when she heard it.

Melisssssa...help.

She sat bolt upright in bed, gasping for air and straining to see into the shadow-engulfed corners of her dark bedroom. *What the fuck was that?*

She crept out of bed and opened the door to her room as

slowly and quietly as possible. The hallway was empty and dark, the only illumination coming from the small plug in light on at night. She was so distracted by mind-numbing fear that she didn't think to flip on the light in the hallway, instead stepping cautiously out into the corridor with its limited illumination.

As she struggled to get her breathing under control, she heard it again, this time very clearly emanating from the closed attic door. It was the first time that the voice/noise/whatever it was had seemed to come from any one place. Though her heart beat so hard in her chest that it hurt, she couldn't stop herself from reaching up and opening the door. She needed answers.

She pulled gently on the handle and jumped back about five feet when the door released with a sharp jerk. It had been a while since she had opened it, and evidently the previous owners hadn't kept on top of oiling the hinges.

She eyed the open door, psyching herself up to pull it the rest of the way, releasing the ladder that was folded up inside. Melissa realized her mouth was open, as if she'd been screaming but no sound had come out. She tiptoed forward and grabbed the handle again.

Like ripping off a bandaid, she told herself, and yanked downwards. The ladder clattered downward, the noise echoing in the eerie stillness of the hallway. If it was possible, her heart rate doubled up, galloping against her ribcage.

Ascending the ladder in the dark, she let out a sigh of both relief and exasperation from she breached the top with just her head—feet still firmly halfway up—and found the attic just as empty as it always was. Her head dropped forward and she let her forehead land with a dull thud on the attic floor. Frustration and fear competed for dominance within her, and she glanced around to find her footing and head back down the ladder when she saw it.

A glimmer of light shone just out of the corner of her eye. Her head whipped around and there it was, an ornate gold mirror. Floor length, on a hinged stand so it could be tilted up or down. The moonlight from the small attic window reflected across the room.

Melissa gasped for air when she realized she had not taken a breath in several seconds, then she hurried down the ladder as fast as possible. Jumping the last few rungs, she hit the floor hard, pain spiking up her calves from the impact.

She wrenched open the door of the nearby linen closet, grabbing a sheet, then scrambled back up the ladder. Heedless of her discomfort with the attic, she rushed across the floor and tossed the sheet over the mirror. She couldn't say, in that moment or any other, why she was compelled to cover the mirror, but she was consumed with the need to do so immediately.

After her headlong rush down and back up again, she stood panting in the middle of the dark attic. The only illumination was the silvery light streaming in through the small, oval window set high in the far wall. She stared hard at the shape outlined under the sheet, questions and fears swirling in her mind.

I'm never going to sleep again, she thought.

She headed back for the opening in the floor, glancing over her shoulder several times to check and see if the mysterious mirror was still there. Every time she looked, there it was, despite her surety that the attic had been empty before. The solid presence of the mirror seemed looming now, as if it took up more space than its dimensions allowed for.

With a final trembling glance as she gingerly stepped down the ladder, she eased herself to the bottom and quickly lifted the door, shoving it closed harder than was strictly necessary.

The next morning before she left for work, she crept up the ladder, both needing to know and terrified of the answer. The mirror was exactly where she had found it, still covered with the sheet and looking far less ominous with bright sunlight pouring in on it from the small window. She sleepwalked through the day, bumping into cubicle walls in the office, spilling her coffee not once, but twice. Her mind drifted back to the mirror and its sudden appearance.

After work, she entered the attic once again, this time climbing to the top of the ladder and entering the small room in one fell swoop, momentarily surprised at her own boldness. She crept towards the mirror, gingerly lifting the sheet to look at it. A part of her expected to see the reflection of a ghoul, a monster, or at the very least the ghostly presence of someone else, but instead only her own reflection stared back at her.

Her petrified expression reflected back, a piece of the white sheet she was holding up and the rest of the empty but dusty attic behind her. She stared into it for a few more minutes, her expression slowly changing to one of intrigue and curiosity.

She studied the frame of the mirror, taking in the ornate scroll work carved into it. *Was that gold?* Finally, she tore her gaze away and released the sheet, heading quickly back downstairs.

Upon entering the kitchen, she was surprised to see the clock read 6:32pm, a full hour and a half after she had arrived home from work. Shaking her head in confusion and resolving to check the batteries at a later date, she set about making herself dinner. The house around her whispered and tapped all the while, however for the first time it didn't seem as unnerving as it had before. She almost felt herself moving to the rhythm of the tapping, subconsciously stepping in time with the erratic beat.

SEVERAL DAYS LATER, the phone rang shrilly, echoing through a mostly empty house. The living room, kitchen, bathroom and bedrooms were all devoid of life. The ladder to the attic was pulled down, the square door in the ceiling still open, a black void. Inside the attic Melissa sat crossed legged in front of the mirror, the white sheet that previously covered it cast aside on the dusty floor as she stared rapturously at her own reflection.

The ringing went on, and still she stared. Hours after that there came a knock at the door, tentative at first then more insistent. Melissa didn't move, and the knocking eventually went away. Night fell, and darkness engulfed the attic, silver moonlight streaming in and reflecting off the mirror, lighting up Melissa's fascinated face.

Her stomach rumbled loudly, the noise echoing off the empty attic walls, but she didn't seem to notice. The sheet that had been previously discarded so easily had begun to build up dust, blending into the rest of the dirty surroundings. Strangely, the mirror itself accumulated nothing. No dust, dirt or fingerprints muddied its elaborate surface. It shone as though it had been wiped down with polish and glass cleaner just moments ago.

As Melissa sat in front of it, though, it was evident that she had not been doing any cleaning. Her hair hung in greasy hanks around her face, her eyes stood out from her face, seeming to protrude from the bruise coloured skin surrounding them.

As morning dawned and the first hints of sunlight glinted off the glass of the window, her head fell forward as she nodded off in front of the mirror, having sat there so long she hadn't slept in over seventy-two hours. The light shifted subtly as Melissa snored softly, chin resting against her chest as it rose and fell.

It was dark when Melissa's head snapped up, her neck sore from sleeping sitting up and slumped over. She looked up at the mirror and saw once again, and as always, her own reflection. The same thing she had seen for several days. *How long have I been sitting here?* she thought. Perplexed though she was, she had no desire to stand up and walk away from the mirror. The same lack of desire that had suffused her being for the last several days.

At first, she had only spent a few hours in front of the mirror at a time, though each time she spent longer and longer. And each time had felt shorter and shorter. By the third day she had missed work to stay in front of the mirror, managing to call in sick and fake a cough before eagerly heading back up the ladder to resume her rapturous staring.

Her first hint that something was wrong was when her reflection stood up, and she did not. All at once, she realized the voice was gone. The tapping was gone. The hissing was gone. After so long listening to the noises all around her, the quiet was uncomfortable and unsettling. *I hate it,* was the first thought that popped into her head.

Her reflection stood, looking down at her as she sat, dumbfounded, her heart pounding in terror. Suddenly, after so many days of being addicted to the mirror, she wanted nothing more than to get away, but fear and horror now rooted her to the spot.

She stared up at herself, her mouth agape in shock. Her reflection smirked at her with a wink and turned towards the still open door out of the attic. As the edges of her vision began to fade to black, she heard a chorus of whispers say *Welcome...*

The attic door closed as the mirror faded out of existence once more.

10

THE FALL

LUCILLE BANE

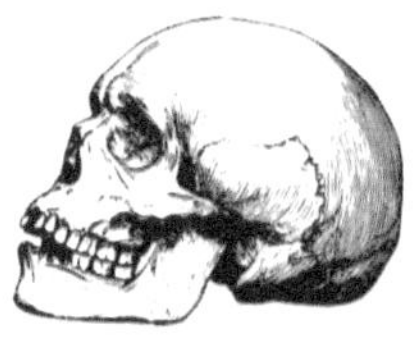

I WOKE UP SUDDENLY, SHIVERING IN MY FRIGID APARTMENT. There was no doubt in my mind what woke me, and I sprang from bed like a gymnast. I dashed around my tiny studio apartment, checking and double-checking every window. Once I was positive they were secure, I poured myself a big glass of whiskey, wincing against the burn as I drank the whole thing. I placed it on the crowded counter, not even bothering to try the overfilled sink.

My place was beginning to stink, the smell of unwashed dishes and unwashed body building seemingly by the hour. I couldn't even remember the last time I showered. A quick coating of baby powder is all I bothered with now, but it didn't do much anymore. My skin is becoming greasy and grubby, my hair limp with oil. I barely left the house now—sunny days were too hot, rainy days were impossible. I couldn't risk it.

My biggest problem now was the rapidly dwindling food supply. I was down to half a pack of crackers and one questionable egg. I knew I'd have to go out soon—I needed supplies. Food, more whiskey, toilet paper, new clothes.

Mine were filthy, as I stopped doing laundry weeks ago. I tried to wear as little as possible, but the frigid air inside made that a challenge.

I watched the rain hitting my window and shuddered. I wish I knew what had happened to me. I went from living a normal happy life to this, practically overnight. The fear was all-consuming, rearranging my entire existence. It was inescapable. The enemy was everywhere. On every street, in every store, even the air was potentially toxic.

I know everyone has fears, phobias even, but this felt bigger. I am genuinely convinced something horrible will happen if I let it touch me, so my every waking moment is spent avoiding it.

Now, at this point most people would say, "Okay, so you have a fear, just avoid that thing and move on."

That's what I'm doing though. The problem is, the thing I'm afraid of is everywhere. I can hear it pattering on my window, gurgling in my pipes, churning beneath the cars in the street.

You see, the thing I fear, more than anything in the world, is water.

The very thing we rely on to survive is the same thing that is gradually destroying my entire world.

It wasn't like this before. Hell, I was on my high school swim team.

Then one morning, I woke up terrified. I don't even recall a nightmare, just chest-crushing dread. That was the day I stopped touching it, drinking it, being anywhere near it. I don't even allow myself to sweat anymore, just in case. Not that I even could, my dehydration is so extreme.

I know I need to go out today, but the rain might as well be a prison guard. I've thought about calling for help. My best friend, or my mom, but no one would ever believe me. They'd say I'm crazy, and maybe I am.

I can't be committed, though. If I end up in a hospital, the first thing they'll do is wash me and give me IV fluids. Could you imagine injecting me with it? The consequences would surely be catastrophic.

Exhausted by my racing thoughts and crippling anxiety, I trudge back to bed, praying the rain won't keep me awake.

When I finally wake hours later the sun is blazing, high and warm. I know this is my chance, today is the day.

Donning my high boots, a loose skirt and a flowing top I steel myself to leave. After twenty minutes of self pep talk, I finally march out the door, determined to get some food. I try desperately to ignore the stares of other people, knowing how I look and smell. The first beads of anxiety sweat tickle and burn beneath my arms.

I have to get this done.

No more than a block from my place I hear the boom of thunder. I dig frantically in my purse for my umbrella, to no avail. The desperation hits me like a truck, and I drop to my knees on the crowded street to dig deeper in my enormous bag. Another rumble of thunder, and I flip my bag upside down, spilling the contents all over the dirty sidewalk. I tear through them like an addict searching for a fix.

Then, with no further warning, the rain begins to fall and I begin to scream.

I try fruitlessly to cover myself, but still the drops hit me. After what feels like an eternity, I realize nothing bad is happening. Everything is okay, it's just a little rain after all.

I rise, laughing, and tip my face up to catch the cool water. It's been so long that the refreshing liquid feels bizarre on my skin.

Suddenly, a woman to my left screams. I turn to look at

her just as another person shrieks. A man in a suit looks in my direction and immediately breaks into a run. There's another unusual sound, like a piece of meat hitting a counter.

Looking down, I see a lump of flesh on the ground. As I stare, confused, another large chunk falls near it. I lift my arms, the skin dripping off of them like melting wax. I try to run but my legs buckle beneath me. I have no choice but to simply sit and allow the water to destroy me, just as I knew it would. I hold on to consciousness just long enough to see my foot come free from my body and wash into the gutter. Then the darkness comes and I know nothing else.

RUN

BRIDGET EILIS

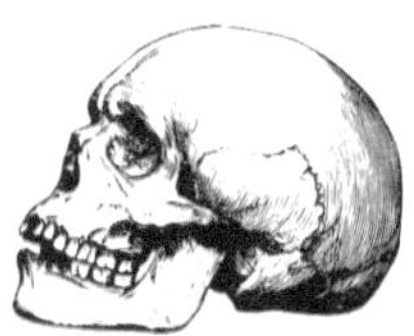

RUN. DON'T STOP. KEEP RUNNING. CAN'T STOP.

This refrain has kept me alive for as long as I've been here. Days? Months? A year? I don't even know. There's no light, no sun, nothing to mark the passage of time. I sleep when I think it's safe to stop for longer than a moment. It's never long enough.

I don't know how I got here, or what is chasing me. All I know is the bone-deep certainty that if it catches me I will die. Eaten, torn up, or some other manner of horrifying end to my relatively young life. That seems unfair doesn't it? I didn't do anything to deserve this.

I'm out of breath, and stop for a moment to lean on... something. Is it a wall? A tree? I can barely see my hand in front of my face, let alone any features of the landscape of hell I'm trapped in. I've tripped, stumbled and fallen so many times I've lost count. My hands are bruised and covered in dried blood. My shoulders and shins are so sore I've forgotten what it feels like to not be in pain.

Roaaaarrrrrr! The noise rends the air behind me, cutting through it and right into my soul.

Run. Don't stop. Keep running. Can't stop.

I pick up the pace again, only to trip over something hard on the ground in front of me. My poor abused hands take the brunt of the fall and I spring back up as fast as I can, faster than I would've considered possible before this nightmare began. Before I can take off again, I see the first glint of light in who knows how long and look down at what I fell over.

It's metal, long and smooth. I pick it up, oof it's heavy. It's a sword, nothing too ostentatious. Not like the ones the heroes carry in movies and tv shows. Just a plain broadsword. Pointy at one end with a smooth leather wrapped pommel.

As I heft the weapon up close to my face to examine it in the darkness, a strange feeling settles inside me. As sure as I have known that if the monster, creature, whatever it is catches me it will be my end, I know that this sword means that end is coming. This is my only hope of defence against it. I've never even held a sword in my life, how am I supposed to-

Rooaarrrrrr! It's closer and I don't have any more time to think about the sword, or anything else.

Run. Don't Stop. Keep Running. Can't stop.

I take off again, dragging my only hope of survival with me. As I move, I get used to the weight of it faster than nature would allow. I know this, but I am soon charging forward, sword held out in front of me as if I've done this all my life. As that thought crosses my mind, I stop. For the first time, I stop not because I am too exhausted to go on, but because I am suddenly struck by the idea that I can fight this. I can win.

"You know, I'm really tired of this," I say out loud the first words I have spoken in recent memory. I don't even know

what it is I am tired of. Is it the running? Is it the continuous definitive surety of these things that keep imposing themselves in my brain?

Don't run. Stop. Can't run. Fight.

I turn and face the beast. I still can't see it but I know it's there. I can hear it, feel its hot breath. I know where it is in the inky blackness with the honed instincts of a lifelong warrior.

I swing the sword with both hands, and it bites deep into the monster's flesh. It screams and reels back. I press forward, striking again and again. It cries out and shrinks away from me, trying to run but I am ruthless. I hack at it until there is nothing left but a pile of chopped flesh and bone, swimming in a widening pool of blood.

I am panting again, from exertion and elation in equal measures. I did it. I don't have to run anymore, I can sleep. I walk a short ways away and sink down against something hard and cool, and lay my sword at my side. My saviour. I drift off easily—I'm so tired.

My eyes snap open and I sit up quickly, frantic. Light pours in through my bedroom curtains.

My alarm blares next to my head and a voice from down the hall calls out, "Are you going to turn that off or what?" I reach for my phone instinctively—I know exactly where it is without looking. The same place it always is. I hit the stop button and the alarm quiets.

It was all a dream, holy shit what a dream though!

Something smells strange in the room with me. I can't put my finger on it but it's a familiar smell, and I turn my head to find the source and there on the bed beside me lies my blood covered sword, stains slowly seeping into the blankets.

That's when the screams begin.

12

MUNCHIES

ALICE J. TAYLOR

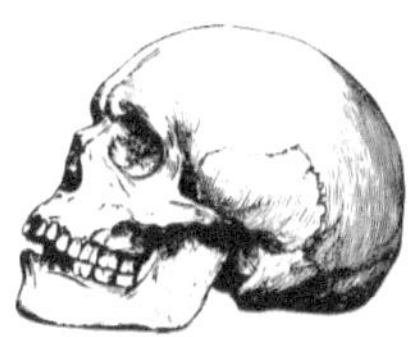

Every night, when I've made myself into a comfy little burrito in my bed, I near noises in my kitchen. It doesn't seem to matter what time I go up to my room, be it evening or the wee hours of the morning, about an hour after I'm in bed, there are noises.

It sounds like...cooking.

Cupboards open and shut. Pans clank. Cutlery clinks. The hiss of boiling water sizzles when it hits a hot element.

When I get up in the morning, everything is in its place. Either nothing is actually happening in there and I'm just imagining it, or I have a ghost that meticulously cleans up after a midnight snack.

Of course, I could go down there and check, instead of quivering in my burrito. But I live alone, man. I've seen enough horror movies to know that it would be *stupid* to go down there and check. There could be anything down there.

It could be a ghost that likes to cook. It could be a ghost that wants me to *think* it likes to cook, drawing me out of my safety blanket and into a grisly death. It could be a monster that wants me to think that it's a ghost that likes to cook, drawing me out of my safety blanket and into a grisly death.

I've been over all the possibilities, trust me. And I'm not willing to risk said grisly death.

So I wrap myself in my burrito, making sure I'm nice and secure on top of my mattress so nothing can grab me from under my bed, and night after night, I wait. I wait for the noises, and I strain my ears to make sure that whatever it is isn't coming up the stairs to kill me. And then, when it finally dies down and my house goes quiet, I go to sleep.

But it's shitty sleep, man. You know when you have a really important appointment in the morning and you wake up every hour to check the time in case your alarm doesn't go off? It's like that, all the time. I sleep so light and any little shift or noise or wind or creak snaps me awake so fast. My dreams aren't so great either, when I manage to sleep long enough to have them.

It's been weeks. And as I'm brushing my teeth, avoiding looking in the mirror in case some ghostie is back there waiting to jump out at me, I decide that enough is enough.

I need to either face this thing and figure it out, or move. That's it.

What's the housing market look like right now?

After scrolling real estate listings on my phone in bed, I decide that tonight is the night I'm going to go find out what the hell is in my kitchen.

My resolve wavers as the minutes tick by. Maybe just one more night. I can do it tomorrow.

Creeeeakkkk SLAM!

Jeez, you know, if it waits an hour to make sure I'm asleep, the least it could do is not slam the damn cupboard doors.

Screeee CLANG!

I take a deep breath. I can't do this another night. I can't do this another second. My muscles are so tense I feel like my bones are going to snap beneath them. I can't live like this.

Clinkclinkclink.

I peel back the layers of my burrito, wriggling out of bed. Goosebumps rise all over my body, and I don't know if it's the temperature change or fear. I take my time putting on a pair of fleece pants and a baggy t-shirt, as much to warm myself as to stall my trip down the stairs.

Thonk. Clang.

I reach into the hall closet and pull out a golf club. I wish I was a sword collector. Except if it's a ghost then a sword wouldn't be any better than the club.

But if it's some kind of horrible monster...I close my eyes and take a deep, ragged breath. I don't need to be imagining razor-sharp teeth and claws the size of my head. Nope. Don't need that.

Thunk. Creeeeeak. SLAM!

I plant one bare foot on the top step. I clutch the club so hard that my knuckles scream. Every nerve in my body is electric, hypersensitive.

Swishswish.

Another step. I can't believe I'm doing this. I'm every horror movie's scene one idiot, investigating the noise and getting killed.

Glubglubglub.

No, no I'm not. It's been weeks of this. And I can't afford to move. I need to face this and figure it out. Three more steps. I can do this.

Thud.

My heart is in my mouth. I can barely breathe. I keep my feet flat on the floor as I move, trying not to make any noise. I inch towards the kitchen. The light is on. I'm so cold.

Swishswish.

I stop at the door frame, trying to swallow the golf ball in my throat, breath ragged and painful in my seized lungs. I'm doing this.

Thud.

I leap into the doorway, golf club extended in front of me, eyes squeezed shut, because that's going to help me fight whatever is in here.

"Uh, hey," somebody says.

I slowly open one eye. What the...my other eye opens and I nearly drop my weapon. It's just a guy. He looks kind of like me, actually. Average height, lean. Dark hair and eyes.

"Uh," I squeak at the end of the word. My mouth opens and closes like a fish hoping for food.

"Sorry, dude," the guy says, and his nose wrinkles as he winces, motioning to the smattering of utensils across the counter. "Didn't mean to wake you. I promise I'll clean up when I'm done."

I...*what*? I drop the golf club and the clatter makes us both jump.

He shimmers. Flickers, like a buffering video.

I point at him, finger shaking. "You're a..." I squeak again, voice failing me.

"Yeah, I'm a ghost," he says, almost apologetically. "I used to live here, before you moved in. Died in a car accident. I just get the munchies so bad at night. I hope I haven't been keeping you up."

I don't even know what to say to that. I press my palms against my cheeks as he absently stirs something in a pot with a wooden spoon—*my* pot and *my* wooden spoon—and wonder how the hell he's even doing that. I have so many questions.

The one that I blurt out is, "So you're cool, man?"

You're not going to kill me? You don't want to eat my brains? Drag me to hell? No grisly death?

"Oh yeah, I'm cool," he says, mouth curling up into a big grin. Too big. "But they aren't."

My brow furrows, and—as stupid as the scene one idiot —I turn around. My eyes barely register the dark shapes with the red eyes before they're on me.

I should have stayed in my burrito.

13

BANSHEE

BRIDGET EILIS

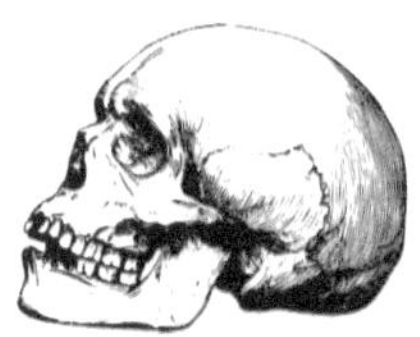

They tracked her for nine hours, by following the blood on the snow before they had to call off the search. Detective Robinson radioed the other officers to let them know. It was dark enough now that they wouldn't be able to follow the trail anyways—best to regroup and pick it up in the morning.

Every police procedural or mystery cop drama had scenes of officers mixed with civilians trudging through the woods in the dark with flashlights, calling out the names of the missing person they were searching for. The reality was much less theatrical. Searching in the dark often led to more injuries than victims found.

As he walked back to his squad car, the dimming light played tricks on his eyes. Shadows moved in ways they shouldn't, and he knew he couldn't trust his depth perception. This time of day, the light always did weird things to his vision. It was the perfect time between day and night—twilight, most people called it—but Robinson had always thought it was a misnomer. Twilight sounded beautiful, it sounded like a fancy way to describe the colour purple. This was anything but that.

He went over the case notes in his head as he walked. Several victims, all male. All of them had their bodies ripped apart. No parts missing; Robinson was glad he didn't have the job of the person who had to determine that. Some of them were at home, some of them in custody. Some of them were even under house arrest, the kind of people who should have been the safest, under the most surveillance.

So how does someone access a prisoner? Surrounded by police officers and concrete walls and metal bars? A person under house arrest? Their movements literally being tracked by the government. How does a man get snatched out of his room in a house full of people and no one else notices, no one else is attacked in the same house?

The suspect was a young woman, early 20's, no record, no history of violence. She was slim, average height. She had natural-looking brown hair—at least it looked like it in the pictures. Women on the force tossed around words like 'lucky' and 'blessed.' Robinson didn't follow the logic, but he assumed it had something to with her natural attractiveness. There was no denying that. But to him she looked like any other suspect, a human being with a number of features to be catalogued. Hopefully some unique identifying feature that would help them in their search.

Somehow, she'd become linked to several murders in the area. Murders of unsavoury characters to be fair, but murders, nonetheless. Brutal attacks. Each victim was left behind mostly intact. Mostly being the operative word, because all of their parts were there. And none of them had any connection to the suspect.

If even one of the cases had some connection to her, maybe

he could've made sense of the case. If there was anything in her past that would explain this. If she were a victim herself, then she could be lashing out at people similar to her own attacker. But even deep-dive research into her background had revealed nothing of that nature. She had no history of violent acts committed against her, no friends in childhood or adulthood that had been victimized. She had no family members that had been killed. Everyone closest to her that had passed had done so of natural causes. She literally had a picture-perfect backstory. The kind of thing that ninety nine percent of the population didn't have. Most people had at least one violent incident in their close family, and almost one hundred percent of women were close friends with an assault victim.

There were several parts of the case that didn't add up to a no-nonsense career cop like Robinson. He'd seen other detectives in his district start conspiracy walls, pinning up pictures and newspaper clippings of unsolved crimes. Some of them were sure there was an outside explanation. They hesitated to say the word *supernatural* because that was a one-way ticket to a psych citation. But the more he mulled over the case, the more he thought there had to be something else going on, some unexplainable force at work.

Every victim was a known murderer or rapist. Several of them had been dragged right out of their bedroom window while on house arrest, or out on bail awaiting trial. In every case, no one else in the vicinity had been injured, even when there were other people just down the hall of the home, or other inmates in the holding cells nearby. No guards or police officers had been injured either.

What he couldn't figure out was how she was doing it.

DNA evidence pinpointed her as the killer—she'd had hers on file from some college safety program she'd participated in. They were very popular at the schools around the city. Fingerprints and photos of every student willing to participate. Sometimes even a video of them walking past the camera and introducing themselves. Unsurprisingly, ninety percent of the participants were female.

However, there were never any weapons found, no shell casings, no bullet holes in anything around the bodies. They seemed to be simply torn apart.

Torn apart by—according to her driver's license records —a woman who was barely five foot six and only one hundred and thirty pounds. He couldn't explain it, nor could any one else who had examined the case. The DNA traces had been found in the wounds of her victims.

The detective stumbled slightly over some concealed roots and redirected his attention to his footing. As he shifted his eyes, he swore he saw the figure of a woman. The moon rose behind her and her body changed into a monstrous form, limbs elongating, fingers stretching beyond any normal human proportions. Her hair grew with an inhuman speed, hanging down her back in long tangled hanks. She hunched over slightly as her spine stretched against the skin of her back. She let out a blood curdling shriek as she rushed towards him, the pitch so high he fell to his knees, hands clasped tightly over his ears to block out the noise. It pierced his skull anyways, and at the same time sharp claws dug ragged fissures in his back and shoulders.

That's how she's doing it, was the last coherent thought to float through his mind, oddly calm as she tore off his limbs one by one.

14

AT ANY COST

LUCILLE BANE

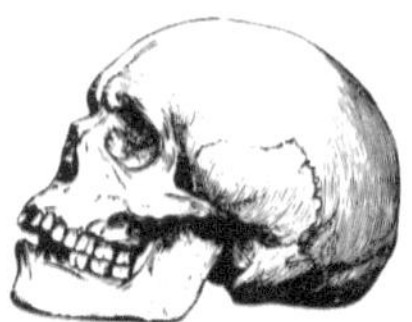

THE MOST SUCCESSFUL SPA IN THE COUNTRY BOASTS OVER TEN thousand elite members and a profit of five million dollars a year. Nestled in a perfect, private mountain location, they closely guarded their flawless beauty secret. They had truly discovered the fountain of youth.

Claire Finn snapped her eyes open when she heard the footsteps. Footsteps were never a good thing. She pushed herself upright, despite the IV line embedded in her chest. Her head spun and she saw white spots before her eyes, but she refused to give in. Claire listened closely but the footsteps had stopped. She strained her ears, only to be accosted by blood-curdling screams. She fell back on her thin cot, both horrified and relieved that they wouldn't be coming for her today.

The spa was packed as usual. Spring months brought the most members flocking in for the treatments and elixir. Everyone wanted to look their best for summer. The elixir was short-lasting, leaving people needing a top up every few months. It was designed that way to keep the members coming.

Claire had long ago lost track of time, but she did know that the footsteps were coming for her. She would do anything to avoid another round with the masked monsters that would soon be entering her cell. The footsteps came closer and she pressed herself against the wall beside the door. They stopped right outside. She gritted her teeth and grabbed onto her IV line.

Bracing herself against the wall, she gave a slow but firm tug, pulling the IV from her chest. Careful not to make a sound, she pressed a shaky hand to the bleeding wound, tightly grasping the needle of the IV in her free hand. She took a deep breath, fighting through her dizziness. The door lock clicked open and she lunged forward as the heavy door swung wide.

She rammed the IV needle deep into the eye of the first person to enter and sprinted out the door. She shoulder-checked the other person with her limited strength and ran in the direction the footsteps always came from.

Her head spun as she focused on the stairs at the end of the hall. She knew she only had one shot at this. She reached the stairs and scaled them two at a time, footsteps pounding behind her. As she climbed the stairs, she spotted a door just ahead of her and prayed it was the right one. She burst through into a pristine white hallway. The brightness nearly blinded her but she forced her legs to keep running. A white-robed person came around the corner ahead just as the door behind her slammed open.

"Help!" she screamed.

"She's stealing the elixir!" the voice behind her called out.

The white-clad person reacted much faster than Claire, and she found herself flat on her back, vision fading fast.

She came to back in her cell, IV lodged back in her chest, this time restrained.

A dark figure stood over her, hooking a machine to her IV. "Nice try, Claire. You know we need that elixir. No matter what the cost."

With that he flipped on the machine. Claire tried to fight but was sapped of energy, as her remaining blood was drained from her body and her eyes drifted shut.

15

DON'T GO IN THE ATTIC

ALICE J. TAYLOR

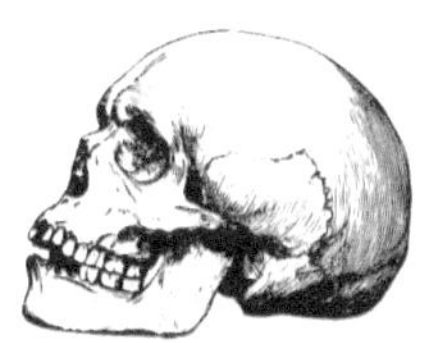

"Auntie Jean, can we go play now?" Frances asked, brushing her white-blonde bangs from her face.

Jean motioned to the open dishwasher from across the kitchen. "You girls clean up your lunch dishes and you can go play. Just don't go up to the attic, understand?"

"Yes mom, we *know*," Angie said, rolling her eyes.

The two young cousins gathered up their plates and cups and put them in the dishwasher with a clatter, squealing and giggling as they tore into the living room like little hurricanes.

"What should we explore first?" Frances asked, clapping her hands together.

Angie rummaged around in her dress-up box and pulled out a pair of safari hats, plonking one on top of her dark curls. "I'll lead the way!"

True to her word, the little girl led her cousin into the dusty sitting room. Her mom had inherited this old house from *her* late aunt, Angie's Great-Aunt Mary, and they'd moved in just the week before. It was a massive old thing, full of ancient furniture and dusty knick-knacks. The girls were ready to explore like their favourite movie archaeologist, searching for rare artifacts and treasure.

"Why can't we go into the attic?" Frances wondered as she peered into a small ornate hanging mirror.

Angie shook her head. "Mom says the floor is too dangerous, it could break and we'll fall through." She picked up a little porcelain cat from one of the shelves and booped its nose.

"But what if there's something cool up there?" Frances lowered her voice. "What if that's where the best treasure is?"

Her cousin shrugged and put the cat back. "There's probably nothing up there if it's so unsafe."

"But what if there *is*?" Frances' eyes grew wide, gleaming with mischief. "We could just peek, right? If we just look through the hole there's no danger. As long as we don't walk around up there."

Angie wrinkled her nose. "You know she'll still be mad if we do that."

"Girls!" Jean called from the kitchen, her voice startling them both. "I'm heading outside to do some gardening, if you need anything just holler!"

Angie cupped a hand around her mouth to yell back, "Okay, mom!"

"Now's our chance!" Frances hissed with excitement as the back door slapped shut. "Let's go! We'll just look."

Her cousin grinned, curiosity finally getting the best of her. "Okay, but hurry!"

They thundered up the stairs to the second floor, then the third. When they reached the end of the hallway, they skidded to a stop on the creaky wood and stood underneath the pull-rope for the attic.

"Together?" Angie asked.

Frances nodded solemnly. "Together."

They wrapped their little hands around the rope, and gave a mighty yank at the same time, drawing down the door. The ladder got stuck halfway down its slide, but with a little wiggling they got it down all the way.

The rungs were wide enough that both girls could fit side-by-side, and so they climbed up that way to have a look around.

They gasped at the sight before them.

The attic was luxurious. Lush crimson carpet spread across the floor, large thick green drapes decorating the walls. A bright gold chandelier hung in the center, hundreds of little prisms sparkling from the metal. A massive four-poster king sat in the far corner, complete with a heavy canopy that matched the red and green of the rest of the room.

Along the side closest to them ran a thick bar with hangers upon hangers of victorian-style dresses, all shining satin and delicate lace. A wide vanity lined with bowls and jewelry and brushes stood next to it, the mirror sparkling as if it had never had a fingerprint on it.

Just like that, the girls forgot the rules, forgot their directive, forgot everything except for the beautiful treasure they'd discovered. They scrambled up into the room.

Frances ran for the dresses, running her hand down a dusty pink ball gown made of the softest silk she'd ever felt. "Who's is this? Look at how pretty it is!"

"Great-Aunt Mary was officially the coolest Great-Aunt ever!" Angie sat down at the vanity and picked up a shining gold bracelet adorned with brightly coloured gems. Before long, she'd put on five bracelets, seven rings, a silver necklace and a gold tiara that was so tall it barely stayed on her head.

She turned around to show her cousin, and saw Frances had put on the gown, complete with matching pink gloves.

"You look like a princess!" Angie gushed.

Frances gave a regal curtsey. "I feel like a princess! You look like a queen!"

They traded places and adorned themselves with everything they could find, eventually dancing around the soft carpet together and then flopping down on the giant fluffy bed in a heap of giggles.

"How long have we been up here?" Frances asked as their laughter subsided.

Angie held her stomach, ab muscles sore from their mirth, and shook her head. "I don't know, but we should go back down before we get caught up here."

"Yeah," Frances agreed, despite a reluctant tone. Neither of them moved.

At the sound of the back door slapping shut again, a fire lit beneath their asses, and they rushed to the trapdoor, pulling clothes and jewelry from their bodies as they went.

"The hats, the hats!" Angie cried as she lowered herself through the door, and Frances skidded towards the vanity to grab their explorer hats. They thundered down the ladder and quickly shoved it back up, giving an extra heave to make sure that the door went all the way closed with the momentum.

They jogged down to the second floor and stopped short, out of breath, as Jean appeared on the landing.

"What are you girls doing? You shouldn't be playing tag near the stairs," she said, and put a work-gloved hand on her hip.

Angie struggled to control her huffing and puffing. "Sorry, mom, we got too into it," she replied. "Are you done in the garden?"

"No, I just started," she said, brow furrowing. "I just forgot my sun hat." She headed into her bedroom and emerged with her straw hat. "You girls should come outside if you want to run around. Come on, let's get you out for some fresh air."

The girls looked at each other and blinked, but inevitably shrugged and headed after Jean, not wanting to give away what they'd been doing or for how long.

Years later...

"Hey, cuz, it's been too long!" Angie squealed as Frances bustled in the doorway with her suitcase. "I'm so glad you could make it."

Her cousin grinned as she shed her coat. "A weekend out in the boonies with my favourite Aunt and cousin? I'll never get too old for Auntie Jean's homemade butter tarts."

"I will be seventy and still eating those things," Angie agreed.

"If you girls would get in here before you stop getting older then you can have some while they're still warm!" Jean called from the kitchen, and the girls headed in from the front foyer.

"This house looks exactly the same as when we were kids," Frances marvelled as she looked around at the rooster wallpaper.

Angie laughed. "Pretty much. Mom always talked about putting Great-Aunt Mary's stuff in storage, but never did. What did you used to call them? *Gaudy knick-knacks?* I guess it turns out you love the same gaudy knick-knacks yourself, eh ma?"

"Oh, tease your old mom." Jean shook her head and

clucked her tongue, pulling a tray of treats from the oven. "See if you get any tarts."

"This is such a cool old house, though," Frances said wistfully, leaning her hands on the island as she sat on one of the stools. "We had fun exploring, eh?"

Angie nodded as she slid into place beside her cousin. "Yeah! Remember that first week when we went into the attic?"

Jean raised an eyebrow, curling one oven mitt and planting it firmly on her hip. "I distinctly remember telling you girls *not* to go up into the attic."

"So many times!" Angie replied, rolling her eyes. "I was sad when you took the rope away and locked it up so that those kids you babysat couldn't get up there. Frannie and I had so much fun that one time."

Her mother wrinkled her nose. "Well now I'm glad I did, since two little girls didn't do as they were told. The floorboards are so weak up there, you could have gotten hurt."

"I don't know how you even figured the floorboards were weak," Frances said with a shrug. "That carpet is so thick."

Jean's brow furrowed. "Carpet? There's no carpet up there."

"Yeah there is," Angie replied. "Great-Aunt Mary had some awesome stuff up there. Old Victorian dresses and jewelry. A big giant bed, too. We ran all over the place and didn't feel a single creaky floorboard, ma."

Her mother's eyes widened. "That's impossible."

Frances and Angie shared a worried glance.

"Girls, there's nothing up there." Jean removed her oven mitts and tossed them on the counter. "I don't know what you think you saw, but the attic is empty."

Frances pushed back her stool and pointed straight up. "Have you been up there since we were kids?"

"No." Jean shook her head. "I did a walk through with the appraiser when the deed was signed over to me, and noticed how unsafe it was up there. I took a quick peek when I locked it up to make sure there were no boxes or any of Aunt Mary's stuff I missed, and it was empty. Haven't been up there since."

"Wait, you looked in there when you took the rope down?" Angie asked, face going pale. "That was a week *after* we'd been up there."

Frances shook her head. "There is stuff up there. Come on, let's go look."

Jean shrugged and untied her apron, tossing it with the oven mitts, and led the curious women up to the third floor. She ducked into one of the spare rooms and came back with a long wooden cane, raising it up to hook into a tiny hole in the trapdoor to pull it down.

The ladder slid halfway and then got stuck, and Jean pulled it the rest of the way. Despite her age, she managed to get up the ladder fairly easily, and her top half disappeared into the hole. The girls held their breath, waiting for the older woman to exclaim in surprise.

Instead, she climbed back down. "See? Empty." She stepped back from the ladder and motioned for them to have a look. "Don't go walking around up there, now. It was bad back then, it's probably even worse now."

"How..." Angie trailed off, and then the two cousins scrambled up the ladder together, just like last time. Being significantly bigger, it was a squeeze for both of them to get up next to each other, but they were so flabbergasted by what they saw that they barely noticed they were squashed together in the open door.

The attic was completely empty. Dusty wood. A dank,

musty smell hung in the air. No carpet. No dresses. No bed. No vanity.

Frances put a hand to her mouth, turning to her cousin. Goosebumps rose on the back of her neck. "What the hell did we play with up here?"

"I don't know," Angie replied, shaking her head. "I don't know." She climbed down, but her cousin stayed there for a moment, taking in the dim space.

She could see it in her mind like it was yesterday. She could feel the silk against her skin, the weight of gold around her neck. The light tinkling of the prisms in the chandelier as they'd danced around beneath it.

She pursed her lips and climbed down to the floor, eyes downcast. "I don't know whether to be creeped out or sad."

"I'm more creeped out that we hallucinated the whole thing," Angie muttered.

Frances crossed her arms. "We did *not* hallucinate it. It was there!"

Jean shook her head and pushed the ladder up, closing the attic door with a loud *bang* that made both girls jump. "Come on, let's go have some butter tarts. Honestly, I wouldn't have been surprised if Aunt Mary had a bunch of Victorian stuff in her attic. She was quite the collector, that one."

As they disappeared down the stairs, voices muffling in the distance, a slender old woman emerged from the shadows of the attic. She spun around, her dusty pink ball gown fluttering, and the dank space erupted in greens and reds, returning to its former lush glory. She sat down at the vanity and picked up one of the powder brushes, swiping a little rouge on her cheeks.

She blew a kiss towards the trapdoor. "Enjoy my knick-knacks, dear niece."

16

GAME OVER

BRIDGET EILIS

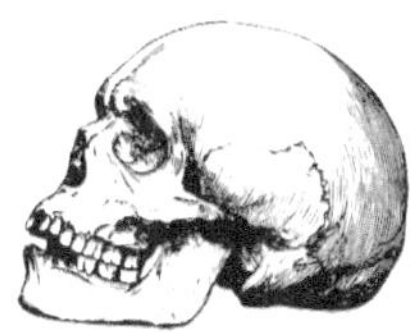

THERE IS NO BETTER WAY TO PASS THE TIME THAN PARKED IN front of a really great video game—I think so anyways. I love to get lost inside a game after a long boring-ass day at the office. There's nothing worse than staring at a computer screen full of mind numbing numbers all day. Unfortunately, accounting pays pretty well, and I have a knack for it, so I deal with the boredom by indulging my hobbies on the weekends.

Sinking into my gaming chair, I put the VR headset on and fire up my beast of a PC. It hums to life with the sound of several fans revving up at once. I navigate the mouse across the screen with the ease and speed of a seasoned gamer—I know exactly what I want and choose the game without hesitation.

Untitled Fantasy Game pops up on the screen in majestic lettering, hinting at the fantastical themes to be found within. I load up my save file—one I've been working on for weeks—and settle in for a good long session.

A few hours later—probably more than I would care to admit—I pull the helmet off, shut off my system and head to bed. It is late Sunday night, and I will probably regret this extended session in the morning, but I definitely needed the time to check out of real life.

I pour my surprisingly tired body into bed and crash hard, hoping for a solid six hours at least before my alarm goes off in the morning.

BEEP BEEP BEEP!

I roll over and fumble around my nightstand for my phone. I deliberately set the most annoying alarm noise I could find—the one most reminiscent of my childhood alarm clock—in order to force myself out of bed in the mornings. I find the phone and silence the noise, rolling back against the bed with a groan. I hate mornings.

Forty five minutes later I am ready to leave for work, dressed like a businessman and not a gamer. I head out the door to meet my Uber driver.

In the backseat of the car, I rest my head against the upholstery and close my eyes. I'm still tired—up too late last night—but I wouldn't trade my gaming time for more sleep, it's not worth it.

Suddenly the driver hits the brakes, and my neck whips forward, hard. I snap my eyes open and in the middle of the road stands an ogre, uncannily similar to the ones from my favourite video game.

The driver screams, and I start yanking on the door handle. This giant monster-like thing stands right in front of our car, raising a large club.

I can't seem to make the door handle work, and when I frantically look back out the windshield, the car starts to move again and all I see is traffic ahead of us. "What the fuck was that?"

"An ogre obviously," says the driver, and when he turns to grin at me over his shoulder I notice for the first time that he has the same face as an NPC my character met in game yesterday.

Did he look like that when I got in the car? Did I even look at his face before getting in? How trusting and yet untrusting we have become as a race.

I'm still turning all of this over in my head when the car pulls up outside my office building, and the driver hands me a debit machine to swipe my card. Filled with confusion, I tap the plastic against the screen and listen for the tell-tale beep before fumbling with the door handle that I wasn't able to make work during my earlier panic.

The street looks normal. The lobby and elevator also look normal. I'm just about ready to chalk this up to some serious sleep deprivation when the elevator doors open, and people run frantically through the halls. High-pitched screams echo off the narrow walls.

Smoke pours out of the double doors that lead into the office I work in. The doors themselves are shattered so it's easy enough to step through the frames without opening them. My briefcase lays forgotten on the floor of the elevator which is already long gone, packed with panicked employees fleeing the scene.

The destruction worsens as I venture inside. I'm not even sure at this point why I'm heading toward the chaos instead of away. Isn't that the first rule in the movies, only morons head toward the screaming? The flimsy cubicle walls are shattered, scattered around the room in piles—most of them are on fire.

That explains the smoke... why am I so calm?

I pick my way through the wreckage, searching for the source of all the fire and brimstone. I cough and sputter, the smoke choking me out. I try and pull my shirt up over my face to filter out the worst of it. It doesn't help, not really. But it gives me the illusion of doing something rather than just blindly walking into the obvious danger.

I reach the windows, the broken glass crunching under my feet. Leaning over, I peer down to the street below, where my Uber pulled up just moments ago. The scene below isn't the calm yet bustling everyday city life I had just left behind. Trees erupt out of the pavement, and the landscape is half-city, half-forest. Large animals that don't belong roam the streets and the people in business suits run away, but the people in skins and furs look upwards. Some of them have bows and arrows trained to the sky.

I follow their gaze and have only seconds to process what I'm seeing. A monstrous dragon swoops down towards the building—its mouth already open with fire burning in the back of its throat. I'm not sure why I'm not screaming but I stare down the creature as it unleashes a fiery roar in my direction. My skin is on fire, cracking and peeling away from my bones. I collapse, I can't breathe, probably because my lungs are literally toast. My organs boil, my blood evaporates in my veins. *This is the end.*

My vision goes dark, then lights up with bright yellow text on the black background. It reads:

GAME OVER

CONTINUE? YES NO

17

DOPPELGANGER

LUCILLE BANE

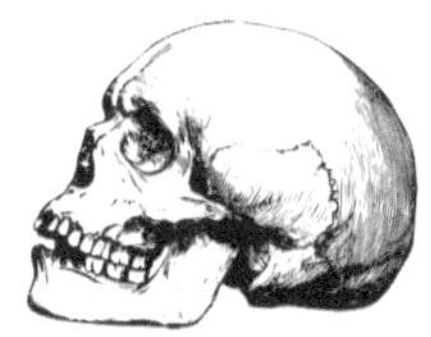

You know that feeling when you look in a mirror, and even though you know it's you, something looks wrong?

That's how it started.

A glimpse in a mirror or a store window that would give me a brief flash of fear. I could always talk myself down. It's just a weird angle, you're tired, the window was dirty. There are plenty of rational explanations for this phenomenon.

What I was struggling to explain was seeing the face in crowds—my face. I've heard of doppelgangers, so maybe that's all this was, some other girl that looks remarkably like me. Who, apparently, is everywhere I go.

The worst moment was a week ago. I finally went on a date with a devastatingly handsome man I met online. We arranged to have dinner and drinks at the nearby pub. The night had been amazing, the drinks and laughter flowing easily. Then I looked over his shoulder and froze.

There she was, sitting right across the bar, staring at me. She didn't just look like me, she was even dressed like me. Ginger hair flowing loosely around her face, sparkling silver eyeshadow drawing out her green eyes. Her one-shoulder black shirt had probably been bought in the same store as mine. I couldn't take my eyes off of her, and my date quickly noticed he had lost my attention.

When he called me out on it I tried to casually draw his focus to her. Yet when we looked up she had seemingly vanished. I spent the rest of the night looking for her and my date rapidly lost interest in my sudden obsession and ultimately, in me.

Now, she was practically stalking me. The coffee shop, the gym, the bar, the park. Everywhere I went, apparently so did she. I couldn't help but see her. In fact, I had begun to look for her.

I saw her at the gym and noticed a change. She stood off to the side, not actually working out, but she looked different. Her skin seemed paler—normally porcelain, it was now nearly translucent. Her eyes looked darker too, no longer emerald green like mine, now nearly black. Was she ill? Should I ask? Was it finally time to approach her?

I mulled over these questions as I finished my set, then stood, convinced I could talk to her. I wiped off my bench, then turned in her direction. She was gone.

In the coming weeks, I continued to see her constantly and I continued to worry about her. She looked worse every time I saw her. Hair limp and thinning, skin practically grey at this point, eyes nearly completely black. I wanted to talk to her, to the point that I was getting a bit obsessive. I looked for her and followed her every chance I got.

I saw her standing outside my favourite cafe one sunny Saturday as I sipped a latte. I left my seat and raced outside, chasing her down the street.

"Wait, please!" I called out to her as she hurried down the street. She turned slowly, so slowly it almost looked painful, and fixed her now completely black eyes on me.

"Go home," she croaked, her voice much deeper and scratchier than expected.

"What?" I questioned, but she simply turned and walked away, rounding the corner of the building.

I ran after her, but when I turned the corner, she was gone. I dejectedly skulked back to the cafe and sat down at my table. It took me longer than it should have to realize my purse was gone.

"Perfect," I muttered, dropping my head to the table.

I spent the next two days cancelling every card I had. By Monday morning, I realized I needed my birth certificate in order to replace all of my ID. I hailed a cab to my parents' suburban home, only to discover they weren't there. I puzzled over that for a moment, before remembering they were at the cottage. I was slightly disappointed, as I'd been looking forward to seeing them. As an only child, I was tremendously close with my parents, so close I actually felt guilty that I hadn't told them about my doppelganger.

I let myself into my childhood home using the spare key they let me keep when I moved out. I stood for a moment in the front hall, soaking up all the sights and smells I knew so well.

I padded up the carpeted stairs, knowing they kept a box of valuables and paperwork in their closet. I found the box easily, so easily that I resolved myself to talk to them about moving it. I sat on the edge of the bed and opened the box. I gingerly started flipping through with the delicate papers and photos.

I stopped suddenly when a peculiar picture caught my eye. It was a photo of my mother in the hospital, clearly taken just moments after my birth. Looking both exhausted and elated as she cradled a tiny baby in each arm.

"What the hell?" I cried out, vaguely noticing the closet door move behind me.

I began examining each paper and photo in the box when I made another jarring discovery. Nestled in behind my birth certificate was another. I pulled them out together, lying them side-by-side on the bedspread. They were identical in almost every way, except the name and the time of birth.

"Rebecca Anne Palmer. Time of Birth: 10:52," I read aloud. I put the two certificates side by side above the picture. My mind reeling and hot tears streaming down my cheeks, I turned back to the box. I quickly found the last piece of the devastating puzzle, a death certificate.

Rebecca Anne Palmer. Time of Death: 13:16

I sat on the bed sobbing, gasping for breath. Suddenly, I felt an ice cold hand on my shoulder. I reeled around and found myself staring at my twin. Skin grey and marbled, eyes black, sunken into their sockets, hair thin and stringy.

I wanted to scream while simultaneously wanting to hug her.

"Come home," she rasped.

"I am home," I stuttered.

"Come home," she gurgled, closing her icicle fingers around my wrist. I couldn't even bring myself to fight as she pulled me into the dark closet, the door slamming shut behind us.

18

NEGATIVE SPACE

ALICE J. TAYLOR

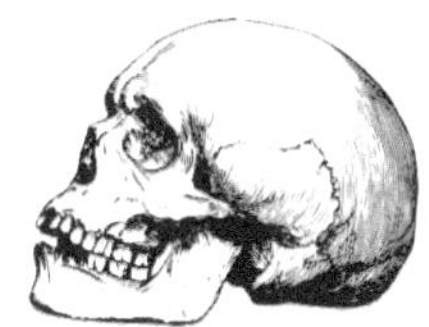

THUMPING BASS RUMBLED IN HER GUTS. EACH KICK OF THE drum reverberated in her bones, the vibrations slapping against each nerve in her body like an ocean swell. Her skin was like napalm, liquid heat engulfing her. Her hips undulated in a rolling crescendo, the music twisting them at its whim.

She threw her head back, blonde curls so soaked with sweat they looked brown, long locks fusing themselves to the exposed skin of her shoulder blades. The bodies around her writhed almost as one, an incandescent sea of flesh. The music splashed over them, through them, under them, creating a pulsing net that held the crowd within its grasp.

Lifetimes passed, entire generations encapsulated in each gyration of her body.

Soon the resonant sounds of bass guitar strings being plucked in a calm euphony caused a soothing energy to fall over the cavernous room, and her movements slowed to a gentle sway. Her lashes rose, revealing french roast eyes that felt like they were opening for the first time.

An emerald green haze saturated the air, illuminating

only distorted shapes and puffs of smoke wafting up like hundreds of tiny volcanoes.

A man towered above the crowd, ebony dreadlocks framing his face like a lion's mane. He held two sticks up in the air, letting out a vicious roar that hung with the profound buzz of the bass notes.

Somewhere, a man howled in response, his exclamation slamming into the roar like a cold front hitting a warm front and the air began to twist and bend and a storm was brewing and her lungs felt like they were going to explode if she didn't shriek and expel the demons inside of her so she opened her mouth and the scream felt like her body was turning inside out like the demon was trying to pull her guts out with it and she was falling falling falling-

The lion's arms bent back at an impossible angle and he cast the sticks into the sea, slick wood flipping end over end in a perfect arc that moved like a tactical missile through the fog and smoke. Each one unearthed an outstretched hand, fingers snaking around timber in a grip that would never let go, for they had found their home.

Electricity danced up her arm upon contact, bones jerking at the sensation of simultaneously feeling empty and full and broken and whole and everything and nothing-

The universe collapsed in on itself and shattered, leaving her in empty whiteness clutching a stick, facing a man left in empty whiteness clutching a stick.

In the distance, a lion's roar thundered towards them, and they fled.

"What the fuck is happening?" he huffed as he ran, feet pounding something hard that neither of them could see.

She glanced behind her, cold gripping at her heart at the thought of the lion gaining ground, but there was only white.

"I don't know," she gasped, head spinning at the thought that they weren't moving away from or towards anything. Her equilibrium thrashed in a violent dance that sent her body sprawling.

His stick halted as if anchored and he let out a strangled cry as his body failed to stop with it. He bounced back like a rag doll and fell next to her. Two panting masses of aching limbs flopped in negative space.

She rotated her head at the feel of his knuckles on hers, half slitting one eye to challenge the vertigo. She focused on the two fists, skin to skin, harbouring lengths of wood and unwilling to let go.

"What the fuck is happening?" she echoed him in a whisper, barely breathing the words into existence.

Dark chocolate eyes fluttered and opened fully, taking in the upside down face of him, all smooth cinnamon skin and amber irises. Terror whirled in his gaze, mirroring her own.

Without any drive or direction, they allowed their bodies to lay in a gnarled yin yang for a time, chuffs eventually descending into soft respiration.

"I can't let go of the stick," she whispered.

I don't want to, and the thought panicked her, so she willed her fingers to uncurl from around the wood and they wouldn't and the wood was life if she let go she'd die she had to keep it forever and ever and-

"What's your name?" His words were like a thunderclap and she startled, pupils dilating, focusing on his lips.

Ignore the white, how are we laying down, ignore the not-ground

Her synapses fired on his question and she frowned. "I... I don't think I know."

"I'm..." His brow furrowed and silence flowed over them

like a river, confusion and panic roiling beneath in violent undertow.

Two bodies splayed in nothingness. The lion forgotten. Lost in the waters of hopelessness, trapped by empty minds.

There was no echo of her agonized screech, the sound swallowed by the white expanse.

sweat soaked bodies writhing together as one/thunder rolling in her bones/tiny squares of paper bitter against tastebuds

"Con-cert," she whispered like a draft between frosted glass.

Understanding clouded his eyes and his gaze was far away, grasping at

hued beams in smoke/the elixir of life contained in clear plastic bottles/flailing kicking undulating

"Concert." The word was hoarse but loud, and the sticks in their hands drew his attention like a magnet. Smooth light wood tapered towards the end, a thin oval bulb topping it like an anorexic snowman.

"Drum." Her vocal chords were compliant and confident in her brain's assessment.

"Drugs!" Excitement flared in his chest, fluttering the membranes of his heart. "I'm high! I'm just high!" Laughter bubbled from his throat like vomit.

Her whole body relaxed into the ground—*not-ground*—a contented sigh escaping her crimson lips. "High. Just high." Glitter infused eyelids closed, relinquishing control to the chemicals flooding her veins.

Confusion.

There was no feeling of electricity, no warmth, no roiling pleasure along the delicate hairs on her skin.

There was no exhilaration, no dizzying vertigo, no colours behind his eyelids.

"I don't..." He struggled to find his words again, brain

cells leaping to grasp the thoughts playing keep away with his rationality.

Her mind seemed to pluck the end of his thought from the cloud, downloading the message and firing it from her tongue. "... Feel high."

What did I take? Tiny squares of white paper adorned with grinning pink cat faces

"Cheshire." His voice shivered and the whiteness shivered and then they plummeted.

They clutched at each other, arms scrabbling for the only other life in existence to hold close as they fell. Terrified eyes darted wildly as flecks of black and grey whipped upward.

Realization crashed over them at the same moment that they still felt as if they were sitting on solid ground. Each hair on their heads weighed down by some kind of gravitational pull unable to be described by the absence of discernible physics instead of flapping wildly above their heads.

"We're not moving." A tentative release of her hand on his arm felt destabilizing, and she gripped him again.

The flecks gradually swelled in size, hazy outlines giving the appearance of inverse stars.

I'm just high, just enjoy it, ride it out ride it out ride it out-

The whiteness bled away as the stars merged completely. Grey globules morphed into sharp contours, black smudges into jagged silhouettes.

Gentle wind caressed skin like a lover's breath and they shuddered together. Soft blades of grass tickled her bare knees, and they were on a lush hill beneath an inky purple sky. Massive shadows littered the dome above, splashed with coloured designs too hazy to make out in the dimness.

Tendrils of yellow light bloomed over the horizon like

long daffodil petals, casting a warm glow across the plush landscape. The sky blossomed into a vivid violet, causing eyes to squint in shock and awe.

The shapes above were vibrant balloons, wicker baskets bumping along underneath. There were no bursts of flame whooshing to keep them on track; somehow they bobbed lazily along with no discernible path.

She sprung up on wobbly legs, adrenaline surging to the tips of her frantically waving arms. He rose slowly as she screamed, catching her drift to connect with another potential living thing.

Colours warped along the surface of the balloons, fish eye lenses scuttling across silk. Her screams ceased, jaw clicking shut, frosty fingers of fear encircling her flesh.

He wanted to inquire, exclaim, demand answers, but no sound would come, and the shimmers solidified into iridescent blue creatures. Terrifyingly beautiful scales of jagged glass, glimmering in the dandelion sun, four spiked legs reaching a barbed tip that defied the probability of tearing the thin material they perched upon. Long hooked tails that coiled up and up, curling into an impossible infinity above a conical head devoid of any semblance of facial features.

Two tiny humans suddenly remembered how to breathe, and drew in simultaneous gasps of air. Each cerulean critter ceased all movement, beaklike noses pointing directly at the source of the ventilation distortion.

In unison they leapt, hovering for a millisecond that felt like a thousand lifetimes, then plummeted towards the grass in whistling nosedives.

Thunkthunkthunkthunkthunkthunkthunk.

A low whine fell from his mouth like a waterfall, body incapable of movement, lacking all fight or flight response that should have been coded into his instincts as if formatted from his hard drive. Creatures scurrying ever nearer, bouncing and flipping back and forth over each other, showing off agility and grace.

Hunters displaying their prowess, prey accepting the futility of fleeing.

The tiny humans clutched each other once again, linked by fear.

I'm going to die holding a stranger. I'm going to die not even knowing my own name.

She thrust her stick hand out as the creatures ascended the grassy knoll. Eyes squeezed shut to the point of pain, pain that would pale in comparison to the feeling of hooked glass tearing flesh and puncturing organs.

Two sets of eyes reluctantly peeled themselves open, widening with awe at the glass scorpions shrinking away from the shaky hand brandishing the stick.

Two tiny humans stood spine to spine, wielding wooden weapons in a sea of serrated scales.

"What now?" He was unsure of whether to try to attack or defend. Would they be stranded here forever on this lush green hill, keeping the monsters at bay with a pair of drumsticks? Would the magic in the sticks wear off? If it did, if they could release their hold on them, would the universe return to normal, throwing them back into the rave from whence they came?

She let out a hysterical and high-pitched laugh that could almost be mistaken for excitement in another circumstance. "No fucking clue."

"You think we can move through them?" He imagined them in a bubble of safety, the membrane made of bulletproof glass, rolling down the hill with creatures diving aside for fear of being crushed.

"And go where?" She didn't sound any less maniacal, nor feel it any less.

"Anywhere." He motioned wildly, ignoring the ridiculousness of purple skies and endless white universes. "There has to be a point to all of this."

"A point?" Another shrill laugh clawed its way from her throat and if he were facing her, she might have stabbed the stick right into his eye socket. Maybe that was the key, the point of it all. Maybe the wood was hungry for blood, and it would release her once saturated in oozing ocular pie.

"I mean, if this is just a trip, then I go and try to make it fun again," he rambled, desperate to occupy his mind with something, anything other than the gods of death dancing around them in a twisted ritual. Talking to her made him feel like she was real, like he wasn't just hallucinating her so that he wasn't alone. "And if I'm not just fucked out of my tree and you're real and this is all real and we were sent here by a magic drummer, then there must be a purpose. Maybe we have to bring these somewhere. I don't know."

She knew he made sense, but her guts were red hot. They didn't have any options. Whatever this was, it was all-consuming, all-confusing, all-complete batshit insanity.

"Go slow," she conceded, reaching back with her free hand to snatch his, her only life raft in a tsunami of hopelessness and fear. His right hand linked fingers with her left, his calloused digits feeling massive against her silky slender claws. They held their grails high, a deformed chandelier descending in a bubble of safety.

Scorpions snapped and clicked and lunged, but kept their berth wide, the bubble descending down the hill through the rustling grass.

They reached the bottom of the hill and ran, legs pumping and screaming, still clutching each other and the totems they'd been gifted from the lion god. Muscles worked overtime, hot and tough as feet pounded dirt.

Two tiny humans reached a shallow river, tinkling cyan water flowing over bubblegum pink stones, something out of a child's drawing. They splashed in, still running, still huffing, and then steaming.

"What is that?!" he chuffed, eyes darting around as their shoes began to hiss.

She stopped short, nearly bowling them both over, and stared down at herself. The pretty water bled dark around her legs. Synapses fired and lungs seized.

"The water's corrosive!" she shrieked.

Two humans, holding hands and sticks, ran through acid water, bringing knees up to chins as they splashed and screamed as their legs burned but they couldn't fall, couldn't succumb any more of their bodies to the river of death.

They made it to the bank on the other side, shoes and socks and pants melted away, skin bright red and blistered in the light of the alien sun.

"We can't—we're gonna die here..." he moaned as they collapsed in the too-soft grass, velvet cradling their searing flesh.

She didn't answer. Couldn't. Her mind reeled, brain pulsed, fear gripped her chest.

And then, the beat of a drum.

The deep bass rumbled the ground like an earthquake, and two tiny humans in a vast world of confusion and horror looked into the forest beyond, gnarled branches like skeleton hands, beckoning as they twitched in the wind.

BOOM.

They simultaneously wondered what size of drum could cause such a ruckus, imagining a giant bearing down with tree trunks on an instrument the size of a shopping mall.

There was nowhere else to go but into the woods, a thin path awaiting them through the trees, flanked by the acid river and the spitting, slicking scorpions beyond.

Breaths heavy, gasping hard, they got to their aching feet, still clutching each other, still white-knuckled on their little sticks, and moved into the darkness.

And dark it was, in that forest, as if stepping into night, complete with the eerie call of an owl, then two, screeches in the inky depths of the woods. They wanted to run, wanted to move, but their feet were made of lead as they staggered down the dirt path, tripping over roots.

BOOM.

Things buzzed around them, things they couldn't see, but the noises were bad enough. With what they'd already seen, the screeches and buzzes and sounds of life conjured up horrendous images, nasty monsters that could leap out of the ebony distance at any time and devour them, tear them apart with razor-sharp claws or gnashing teeth...

BOOM.

"Should we... should we be going this way?" she asked, voice trembling as her skin crawled.

He opened his mouth to reply, teeth clicking against each other as he snapped his jaw shut again. He didn't know. He didn't know anything.

But the drum called to them.

Where else do we go? he thought, and whether she heard it or not, he wasn't sure, but she didn't reply, and they continued to walk.

BOOM.

Closer and closer to the thunderous drum, their hearts and skulls thumping with the bass.

BOOMBOOM.

The trees parted, twisted and dead, leaving two tiny

humans at the top of a cliff face, jagged rocks pointing every which way to reveal the chasm below. At the very bottom was, indeed, a drum, but it wasn't very big, and nobody thumped on it, not even a giant.

They waited. Stared. Tried to make sense of it. Couldn't.

BOOMBOOM.

The drum thrummed all on its own, emanating from its place in the cradle of death, no plants daring to grow amongst the black slate abyss.

As if by instinct, they held up their stick hands, holding up the totems they'd been given, bound to, unable to let go. Something inside, pulled by the guts, jerked every time the drum bellowed its bass beat.

Without a word, they descended. The stone was cold, icy cold, feeling good on their blistered feet for a few seconds until their toes went numb, pins and needles licking their nerves as they tried to navigate the jagged rocks. With no hands, they had only each other, and only their feet, and every time they fell and pulled each other back up, the cold stayed with them. Whatever part of them had contact with the surface stayed frozen, hard, like a lump of frozen meat half-thawed.

BOOM.

The drum grew closer and closer, and so did a mounting feeling of dread. The lumps of frozen meat hardened in their guts, bringing nothing but unease and anxiety. They staggered at the bottom, dragging numb feet and stinging legs towards the ghastly instrument.

It looked like it had been painted with blood, intricate designs along the outer shell swirled with crimson, brush-strokes more like finger strokes than anything else. It stood on a rickety stand made of uneven grey sticks—no, no, those were bones, the drum sat on bones, were they human bones?

"Ohhhhgodd..." she moaned, and she moaned because the skin of the drum was human skin, stretched and still moist, the ragged torn edges dangling off of the sides still dripping blood, tied around the top with some kind of sinew and she knew—just *knew*—that it was from a body, from a human, from a living thing, this drum had been constructed from something *living-*

BOOMBOOM.

This close, the ground rattled, but the drum stayed still, never faltering, never tipping despite the movement of the earth. Two tiny humans stood before an instrument of fresh death, a drum, holding sticks, staring at it, then at each other, then at it again.

"Are we supposed to..." The words catch in his throat. They came here with sticks. Would they leave through the sticks? Or would the simple act of beating his drum unmake existence?

They didn't know.

But they felt like they had no other choice.

"On three," she whispered. Unsure of why she should whisper, but she couldn't help it, the air was too still, too thick, too dangerous to be moved by her noise. "One."

BOOM.

"Two."

BOOMBOOM.

"THREE!" And she found her voice, and they brought the sticks down in unison, slamming their totems down onto slick skin, and the resounding *BOOM* was earth-shattering, everything coming apart at the seams as if they'd just been in a bag the whole time and someone clawed it apart, into tatters, nothingness, spacetime ceased to exist and they screamed and screamed but no sound came-

Lisa groaned and her eyes fluttered open, then immediately closed again.

What the hell?

Sunlight. A cocoon.

Where am I?

She slitted her eyes again, and then the familiar scent of her lavender laundry soap invaded her nostrils, comforting her with a kind of relief that was almost terrifying. She was soaked with sweat. Had she been having a nightmare?

She slithered out from beneath her duvet, brushing her matted bangs off of her forehead. Her bedroom. How had she gotten home from the concert last night? She searched her memory, but everything was just fuzz after her acid had kicked in.

What a crazy trip, she thought, though she didn't quite know why, since she didn't remember anything crazy. But the sweat. Dehydration.

She swung her legs out from under her covers and recoiled. She'd slept in her clothes, and her jeans looked seared off at the knee. Her shoes and socks were gone, and her legs were bright red, as if she'd passed out in the sun and cooked them.

Her heart pounded, then seized, and the air left her lungs. In the back of her brain, she heard a *boom*, as if someone were smacking a bass drum inside the base of her skull. She pressed her hands to her temples, blinking rapidly.

She shook her head, trying to rid it of the cobwebs from her trip the night before. Water. She needed water.

As she staggered to her sore feet, her brow furrowed as

she glanced at her nightstand. Sitting next to her alarm clock was a drumstick. For some reason, she felt like she shouldn't touch it. She wanted to throw it in the trash, get rid of it, get it away from her, but her whole body turned to ice at the thought of even brushing her fingers against it.

"That's cool," she said, to nobody in particular, but mostly to the stick. "That's cool. You can just live there, then."

She staggered to the kitchen, her skull resounding with *boomboom, boom.*

19

DARKNESS

LUCILLE BANE

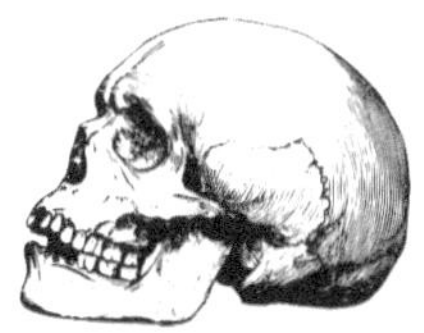

THE DARKNESS CAME WITH NO WARNING. IT FELL OVER THE town like a blanket, shutting out all discernible light. The streetlights didn't even come on. It was all-encompassing, absorbing even the shine of flashlights or car high beams.

Within moments, the street was saturated with the sound of screeching metal and screams of pain. The lights inside buildings had no effect, and soon was as dark as the outside.

The town immediately fell into panic. People tried to flee by foot or in cars, creating more blind chaos. Within hours, the mayor announced martial law would be enforced. Everyone was ordered to be off the streets and stay in their homes. It was the right call—the smartest decision to keep everyone safe.

I heard the news and I was instantly filled with anxiety. I wasn't afraid of the darkness, nor the army patrolling the streets. I was afraid of *him*, and now we were trapped together. My very existence pissed him off and I strived to stay away as much as I could.

Now there was nowhere to run.

I tried to move around as quietly as possible, trying not to alert him to where I was. Maybe if I was careful I could get to bed without incident. Of course, trying to navigate in the dark made it very difficult to also be quiet. I thought I knew where everything was, but without sight I became disoriented.

Realistically it didn't matter how dark it was. He could find me as if he could smell me. Who knows, maybe he could.

I felt a hard pinch on the inside of my arm. It stung like crazy, and I tried to swat him away, but met only air. The shove came next, nearly knocking me over. I didn't scream—I refused to. I wouldn't give him the pleasure. He yanked my hair, scratching the back of my neck in the process. I tried to pull away, to run anywhere.

But of course he was everywhere. He came at me again, managing to push me to the floor. I tried to fight back, but never landed a blow. I knew I never would. I would never survive being trapped with him. I had only one choice.

I stumbled through the house, groping at shelves and walls until I found what I was looking for. The front door! I turned the knob and yanked it open. I ran into the street, hoping to run into an officer. I zigzagged up the road, frantically waving my arms. I heard voices in the darkness ahead, voices that would hopefully save me.

"Hey!" I screamed.

"Ma'am! Return to your house," replied someone from the darkness.

"No! I won't! You can't make me!"

"Ma'am. We have orders to open fire if we encounter defiance!"

I screeched in response. "I'm not going back! You can't hit me if you can't see me!"

I turned. Clearly they wouldn't help me. I heard a strange sound and lost my footing.

When I opened my eyes, I was back in my house. The darkness was still suffocating but I could somehow see through it. I lifted my head and there he was, smiling that twisted away he always had.

"No," I whispered. "Go away. You're dead."

"I know," he rasped. "And now you are too. We'll be together forever."

20

EMOTE THIS

ALICE J. TAYLOR

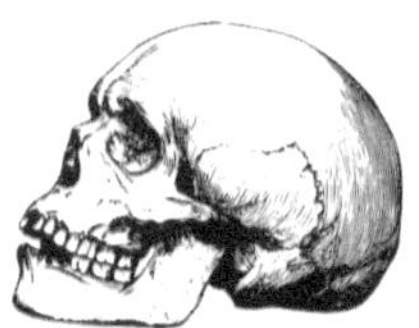

MY PHONE IS FUCKING HAUNTED, MAN. EVERY TIME I TRY TO text someone and hit send it replaces my message with an emoji. And not the cute ones, either.

My girlfriend sends a sexy pic and I reply with a puking face. Now she won't even talk to me. My boss asked me to work an extra shift Friday, and my stupid phone sent back a middle finger. Now I don't have a job. Then my mom invited me over for dinner and she got a Devil face, a fire extinguisher, and a screaming face. Now she's not only not feeding me, but she wants me to see a doctor. And my dad has been bitching at me for two days.

So what the hell? I tried to fill out a contact form on the phone company's web site and all that did was send them a bunch of eggplants. I've been tweeting nothing but heart-eyes and little flames for days.

I really need a new fucking phone. But of course it's Sunday and everything is closed. I'm so bored because nobody is talking to me. At least I can play my games. But I'm so lonely, man.

So I'm scrolling some forums—of course I can't reply,

but whatever—and I get this text from a number I don't recognize. It's one of those auto text numbers, 666-0. Did I forget to pay my bill?

I scowl when I see an emoji. Stupid phone is changing my incoming shit now, too? It's a little spider. Just what I always wanted... NOT.

Out of the corner of my eye, something moves on the wall, and I turn to see a fat black spider crawl out from behind the living room curtain. Now I don't usually squeal like a little bitch over bugs, but dude, this thing is *big*.

I toss my phone onto the couch and head off to dig out my vacuum cleaner. Shut up, I know, I'm not proud of it. But, like, if I squash this thing with one of my shoes it's big enough that it'll leave guts all over the place. Nobody wants guts on their wall or shoe, man.

When I get back from the hall closet, the spider's gone. My lips turn down into a scowl. The only thing worse than a gigantic spider near you is one that you know is hiding somewhere.

Ugh. I move the couch over with a grunt. Nothing. Dammit.

My phone screen lights up again. Same number. Sorry, whoever you are, I can't read your shit because my phone is fucking haunted.

The emoji staring back up at me this time is a flame. Yeah, I'm on fire, bro.

As I shove my couch back into place, my fire alarm suddenly begins to blare, the piercing noise cutting through my eardrums like a knife.

What the hell? The smell of smoke invades my nostrils and I tear for the kitchen. My stove is on fire! I wasn't even cooking anything! I stare dumbly at the flames, my brain slower than my body, and then reflexes take over and I throw open the cupboard beneath the sink, snatching up my little extinguisher. It takes me a minute of fumbling as the flames blister my face, but I figure the stupid thing out and spray with all I've got.

Bottomoftheflamesspraythebottomfuckfuckfuck-

When the can is empty, all I'm left with is a useless smouldering appliance, but at least the fire is out. How the hell did this happen? Was it some kind of electrical thing?

The fire emoji.

The spider.

It can't be.

I drop the extinguisher with a clatter on the linoleum and practically fly back to the living room, picking up my phone just as another text lights up the small screen.

A zombie emoji.

Well that's just not possib-

There's a loud *thump* from my bedroom, and my heart skips a beat. No fucking way. There's just no way there's an undead corpse in my bedroom.

There's muffled moaning and snarling from behind the flimsy wooden door, and then what sounds like a limp hand smacking against it. Nope. Nope. Huge nope.

"How are you doing this?" I demand, staring down at my phone. Can whatever it is hear me? I slide to unlock and rapidly type out a text message.

hey ghost motherfucker stop it right now

I hit send, and all that appears in the messenger app is a sparkly pink heart.

That is definitely not the message I want to get across.

Three little dots appear on the screen. My anticipation is palpable, set to a backdrop of thumps and smacks and groans from my bedroom.

It's a little yellow face with a zipped up mouth. I want to scream.

Except I can't.

Literally.

My mouth won't open. I reach up with a shaking hand to touch my lips. But they're not there. Blood rushes in my ears and I manage to scream, the noise reverberating in my throat, vocal cords vibrating, Adam's Apple bobbing, fear making the edges of my vision blurry and black.

Breathe, breathe, breathe through your nose.

The three dots again.

No. No. Stop.

A butcher knife.

I dive to the floor, as if one of my knives would fly out of the kitchen right into my face. I mean, it probably would, right?

Pain sears my gut, and I grunt as the carpet suddenly feels warm and squishy beneath me. There's a sharp *crack* from my bedroom, but there's no time to worry about that. I'm bleeding, I'm bleeding... I reach down and my fingers brush against a metallic handle protruding from my side.

I roll over, moaning, mumbling—*because I have no fucking mouth!*—and there's a knife in me, oh god there's a knife in me, do I pull it out?

CRASH!

I stare helplessly at the hallway, my bedroom door obliterated, and I struggle to breathe as the smell hits me first. Rotted flesh, the sickly sweet smell of old meat left for bacteria to consume, but it's a humanoid pile of old meat, staggering towards me with its grey-green arms outstretched, black mouth open wide, groaning its excitement at a fresh meal.

The knife!

I don't even psych myself up, I just jerk the knife from my body, swallowing bile at the *squick* as it comes out of me—there was a *knife* in me—and scramble around to slash wildly at the zombie—*zombie!*—coming to eat me.

My phone lights up from the floor and I see the final emoji. I know it's the final one, because it distracts me enough that the monster is able to leap forward and sink its teeth into the rapidly pulsing flesh of my throat.

As my vision goes red and I fall underneath the hungry zombie, my phone taunts me with a skull and crossbones emoji.

21

LOCKED IN

BRIDGET EILIS

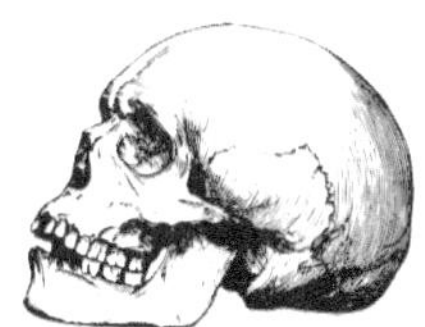

How long have I been here? Have I always been here?

It feels like I was born here, but I know that can't be true. But it is true, isn't it? Sometimes I remember nothing but here.

The windows and doors are boarded up, there's no natural light except through the cracks in the boards. The furniture is old and broken, dust covers everything.

Sometimes though, sometimes I wake up and I see a different place.

No that's not right. The same place, but it is different.

Light pours in through the windows, the doors are thrown open and fresh air pours in. The breeze moves brightly coloured curtains hanging open around the framed double pane glass. On the couch is a blanket, haphazardly tossed there by someone cleaning up.

On the floor, which is clean and free of dust and debris, there are toys and books scattered about. The laughter of children rings through the house. The smell of baking bread wafts from the kitchen, music plays out of the TV in the living room. The furniture is intact, clean and well taken care of. Outside, how I long for outside, where the grass grows lush and green. Cars drive by and dogs chase them as they go.

On these days I wake up and I run, I run through the house as fast as I can to find the source of the laughter. To try and make it outside, into the sun that I can barely remember. I never make it. I trip and fall, only to wake up again in a dusty broken down building, locked in with no hope of escape. Or I get there and the door is already gone, disappearing beneath a pile of boards nailed over it.

On most days I am sure that this fantasy world I sometimes see is an hallucination. A desperate trick my mind is playing on me to stave off insanity. But if I've always been here, am I already insane? Or am I immune since this is where I belong, and where I've always been? I'm desperate for answers, but none ever come.

On other days, days that seem to be fewer and farther between, I am sure that the fantasy is my reality. The place I really belong, and where I am supposed to be. I remember vividly the faces of the children that produce that laughter. I remember reading them books, singing songs with them, feeding them the bread that is always baking in the oven.

Which one is it? Where do I belong? How long have I been here? Have I always been here?

I wander through the house, both alien and familiar at the same time. I wonder when was the last time I ate anything. Shouldn't I have starved to death by now? I try to turn on the taps but all that comes out is liquid rust, sputtering and spraying me with dirt.

Sometimes I spend hours, maybe days banging on the inside of the boarded up windows. I punch and kick the wood until my hands are broken and bleeding. I scream for someone, anyone to please find me, save me, anything. My throat is aching, my voice hoarse from overuse.

I sit on the broken bed, chipped paint flaking off the walls all around the room. Thick dust coats the floor, my footprints have left imprints from the door to the place where I sit now, head in my hands. How long have I been here? Have I always been here?

I HEAR the familiar screams from upstairs and run up to make sure she's okay. I jump over toys and books that the children have scattered across the room. They have abandoned them in favour of the backyard.

It's springtime and the green grass has finally come back —they've left the back door open in their haste but that's okay, the fresh air is nice as it breezes through the house. The curtains that she put up so long ago rustle in the wind.

I reach the top of the stairs and there she is, my beloved Laura, my wife.

She's screaming at something I can't see, because of course it's not there.

I take her wrists gently in my hands and hold them away from her face so she doesn't hurt herself again. She looks into my eyes and for a moment it's almost like she recognizes me.

"Laura?" I ask, but the moment is gone, she retreats back into the madness that took her.

22

THE FOREST

LUCILLE BANE

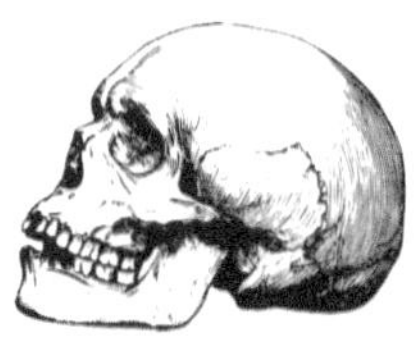

"Are you sure about this?" Shane asked nervously. "Seems kind of dangerous."

"Aww, muffin," Raven mocked. "You're afraid of the big bad forest?"

He looked at her in the shadowy darkness. At barely five foot four inches, with short blond hair and delicate features, she looked more like a fairy than a grown woman. However, in the few weeks he'd known her, he had discovered she was not as innocent as she looked. In fact, she was completely unpredictable.

Nonetheless, he had heard things about this forest. Disturbing things. Everyone seemed to have a story about these woods. Weird noises, strange shadows, even disappearances. Which made no sense at all. The forest was only three blocks long, with a road running so close on the south side you could hear the cars driving by. It would be impossible to get lost, even at night.

The stories must be exaggerated, he thought.

He looked at Raven, who was clearly becoming impatient.

"So?" she asked, grabbing his hand. "Do you want to get a little dangerous? Or are you too scared?"

He rolled his eyes at her sass, then grabbed her around the waist, pulling her up on her toes to kiss her deeply.

"Let's go," he growled, pulling back. He let her lead, already knowing that she preferred to be in control.

She darted ahead, slipping between trees, dancing in and out of shadows. He caught up to her at a boardwalk bridge spanning a small creek. She sat atop the wood railing, the look in her eyes practically ravenous.

"Right here?" he asked, skimming his fingertips up her bare thighs and under her skirt.

"Right here!" She grinned, grabbing his shirt and pulling him to her. With her hot tongue in his mouth and firm body wrapped around his, he quickly forgot about their unnerving location.

Twenty minutes later, Raven sat up. Drenched in sweat with pine needles stuck in her hair, she looked at Shane in amazement. "Holy shit, you're strong."

He gave her a lazy half-smile, pushing himself up from the mossy ground. "Why here?" he asked. "Surely you've heard the stories."

"Of course I have." She smirked, getting to her feet. "That's why. It's exciting when it's a little dangerous."

"So you believe the stories?" he asked, standing up and fastening his belt.

"How could I not? Listen." She held a finger to her lips. They fell silent, listening to the forest shift and rustle around them. Suddenly, there was a deep growl from a throng of nearby trees.

His eyes widened as he whispered, "What the hell was that?"

She smiled mysteriously as she took a step closer to him. "You know what I've heard? This forest isn't haunted with regular ghosts. It's a demon! And once that demon picks a person, they have to give it whatever it wants if they want to survive."

"What does it want?" he asked, heart pounding uncomfortably in his chest.

"Blood, of course. But not just any blood. Blood rich with oxytocin, dopamine and endorphins. The best way to achieve that is..."

"Sex," he interrupted, voice shaking.

The growl came again, closer this time.

"They say people disappear in here. You have to wonder if they get lured out here for sex, then sacrificed." She grinned, enjoying his clear discomfort.

He stared at her, wide-eyed for a moment before speaking. "You don't really believe that, do you?"

He looked over his shoulder as the trees rustled and creaked.

"You don't? Where did all those people go, Shane? No one gets lost in here. There's got to be something going on."

"Maybe you're right," he said, moving closer to her. "We should get out of here."

The growl came again, no more than 10 feet away this time.

"Why? Are you afraid of little old me?" she teased.

"Not at all," he rasped, lunging forward. He wrapped his large hand around her tiny throat and spun around, putting her between the trees and himself. "You're a clever girl, but far too daring," he hissed in her ear.

He reached into his pocket and pulled out his trusty

switchblade. A large black creature with red eyes stepped out of the trees at the exact moment Shane cut her from ear-to-ear.

He grinned at the massive demon. "Dinner is served."

THIS IS the end of this anthology, but if you're hungry for more, grab Don't Read This Book After Dark: Volume 2!

ABOUT THE AUTHORS

BRIDGET EILIS *(Emerald Baynton)* is a homeschooling mom of two and author hanging out by the ocean on the East Coast of Canada. She fills her time between lessons writing, crocheting, and experimenting in the kitchen. And of course, watching Star Trek reruns with her husband.

Find Emerald and her collected works at www. emeraldscreations.org.

ALICE J. TAYLOR *(Emily S Hurricane)* is an east-coast Canadian mama of two that enjoys crafting and baking and writing to keep herself sane. Her hundred-year-old house is probably not haunted, but who knows?

Find Emily and her collected works at www. emilyshurricane.com.

LUCILLE BANE is a single mom from Southern Ontario. Born with a love for all that is dark and creepy, she is naturally drawn to the horror genre. When she's not working, shuttling kids to sports, or hitting the gym, she likes to curl up with a hot coffee and let the monsters out.